When she looked up into his eyes, she found them dark with worry and frustration.

"You can't do anything," she reminded him. "Not in an official capacity. And unofficially, no one is going to talk to you, Ben." She gentled the assertion with a wan smile. "They don't know you." He was an outsider and always would be. No matter how welcome they said he was.

With a rumbling growl of frustration, he yanked on her hand, pulling her up against the solid wall of his chest.

"Do you always have to be right?"

She raised a shoulder. "I can't help it."

"And I can't help this."

He pressed his mouth to hers, crushing her lips beneath his.

AN ABSENCE OF MOTIVE

MAGGIE WELLS

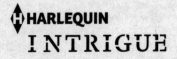

For Michelle. You dreamed my dreams for me, then encouraged me to chase them. You cheered me on at every step, brushed me off when I got knocked down and remain staunchly by my side even from the other side. Our friendship was written in the stars.

HARLEQUIN®
INTRIGUE®

ISBN-13: 978-1-335-48906-7

Recycling programs for this product may not exist in your area.

An Absence of Motive

For questions and comments about the quality of this book, please contact us at CustomerService@Harlequin.com.

Harlequin Enterprises ULC
22 Adelaide St. West, 40th Floor
Toronto, Ontario M5H 4E3, Canada
www.Harlequin.com

Printed in U.S.A.

By day **Maggie Wells** is buried in spreadsheets. At night she pens tales of intrigue and people tangling up the sheets. She has a weakness for hot heroes and happy endings. She is the product of a charming rogue and a shameless flirt, and you only have to scratch the surface of this mild-mannered married lady to find a naughty streak a mile wide.

Books by Maggie Wells

Harlequin Intrigue

A Raising the Bar Brief

An Absence of Motive

Visit the Author Profile page at Harlequin.com.

CAST OF CHARACTERS

Marlee Masters—Newly minted attorney whose controlling father is railroading her into coming home to take over the family business.

Ben Kinsella—Former big-city DEA agent turned rural county sheriff. With his cover blown and a bounty on his head, he's trying to find some peace and rebuild his life.

Lourdes (Lori) Cabrera—Masters County sheriff's deputy and Ben's right-hand person. She was romantically involved with Marlee's brother at the time of his death.

Henry Masters—Marlee's loving but overbearing father. President of Timber Masters, the county's biggest employer, and most influential man in the area, Henry is used to getting his way.

Carolee Masters—Marlee's mother. Fragile and heartbroken by the loss of her only son, she uses alcohol to numb her pain.

Wendell Wingate—The Masters family attorney and Marlee's mentor. He's about to campaign for a seat on the Circuit Court bench.

Will Thomason—Henry's second-in-command at Timber Masters, he has stepped in to fill the shoes of Marlee's deceased brother.

Jeff Masters—Marlee's late brother was involved with Deputy Lori Cabrera at the time of his death.

Chapter One

The only thing Ben Kinsella ever wanted to be when he grew up was nothing like his father. It was the truth, plain and simple. Some boys wanted to be firefighters or doctors or astronauts, but he honestly couldn't remember ever giving those professions a second thought. Or any occupation in particular. He only wanted to be something more than "no damn good."

So far, he'd succeeded.

Glancing down at the khaki uniform he wore, he grimaced and brushed away the evidence of the cruller he'd wolfed down. There were moments when he could not imagine why any young boy would ever think growing up to be a police officer would be a good idea.

"You all right, Sheriff?"

Julianne Shields, Masters County's clerk/dispatcher/secretary, remained unruffled, as always. Unlike him, the woman was a fixture in the boxy building serving as both the town hall and county offices. He hadn't had to call her to come in. She'd shown up minutes after dawn with a box of the tasty treats—still warm from the fryers at Brewster's Bakery—and started running interference for him.

It hadn't simply been a long night. Two days had rolled into one since Clint Young's mother had called to say her son had never returned from his fishing trip. A quick drive out to the property on Sawtooth Lake later, one of Ben's deputies discovered Clint's lifeless body sprawled across a broken-down sofa in his family's old cabin.

The Youngs' place was little more than a shack, but there was a tricked-out Charger parked on the dirt lane leading straight to the door. And Clint's clothes weren't cheap either. From what Ben observed, they were blood-splattered but pricey. A fella didn't grow up in Ben's old neighborhood without knowing exactly what a trendy pair of kicks cost.

Deputy Schaeffer, a former classmate of the deceased, rambled on and on about Clint having "finally gotten himself together." From what Ben could decipher, Mike believed the victim's steady job as a foreman at Timber Masters, new car and nicer clothing meant the guy was really making it. He supposed he would have thought the same thing at Mike's age. He made a mental note to give the car and clothes more thought in light of Clint's financial circumstances but set those details aside in hopes of securing what was left of the alleged crime scene.

Unfortunately, his deputy hadn't handled the discovery with as much professional detachment as Ben would have preferred, but he couldn't blame the guy. The grisliest scene Mike Schaeffer had seen in his twenty-two years was a three-car accident out on Route 32. He'd never seen a person's insides splattered around like a paintball shot. But Ben had.

Closing his gritty eyes, Ben inhaled deeply and said a prayer the coroner didn't suspect foul play, because his deputy had compromised the crime scene beyond any hope of excavating clear evidence. Still, they'd done what they could.

"Sheriff?"

Ben's eyes popped open. His other deputy, Lourdes Cabrera, appeared in the doorway, and not for the first time, Ben wished Lori had been the one to discover Mr. Young's body. Though she was roughly the same age as Mike and the deceased, Deputy Cabrera was calm and cool. Unflappable. She was former military police like Ben. Establishing order was the first point of business on any scene, and the scene the previous night had been chaos. Mostly because Mike was too young and too green. "Hey, Lori," he said tiredly.

His deputy stood with her hands braced on her hips above her nylon utility belt, an old-fashioned glazed doughnut pinched between her fingers. For one groggy moment, he wondered if she planned to tase him awake.

"Why don't you run home and grab an hour or two, maybe a shower?" The expression of concern she wore undercut the stridency of her suggestion.

Scrubbing a hand over his face, he nodded, grimacing as the stubble rasped his palm. Not only did he feel awful, he probably looked warmed-over. "Yeah, I, uh—"

He trailed off, patting various piles on his desk. He

wanted there to be something useful in one of them. But there was nothing. And there wouldn't be anything until Mel Schuler, the county's coroner/funeral director, determined whether the body needed to be referred to the state medical examiner for further testing.

All too aware he was stuck until then, he pushed back from the desk. "Mel should be calling soon," he said.

Lori nodded once. "I'll call you the moment I hear from him."

"Even if it's only an hour or two from now," he interjected sternly. "I need to know what he says more than I need sleep."

Her lips twitched into a smirk as she toasted him with the doughnut in her hand. "Even if it's thirty seconds after you walk out this door, I'll call," she promised, then she took an enormous bite.

"You're only playing into the stereotype there," he grumbled as he sidled past her into the outer office.

"Says the man who demolished two crullers before he even hit his desk chair," Julianne said without looking up from the report she was typing.

"Hey, now, it's not fair picking on me when Mike isn't here to even up the sides." He'd sent the shaken man home directly after he'd recorded his notes for Julianne to transcribe. Ben gave a tired chuckle as he reached for the ball cap emblazoned with the department logo from the coatrack by the door.

He'd just pulled the brim down low when the front door banged open and Henry Masters burst in. Ben blinked hard, willing himself into a more alert state as he rolled his shoulders back and plastered on a pleasant expression.

Henry Masters was the man who'd hired him. One of three men serving on the Pine Bluff town council, he was the owner of Timber Masters, the great-grandson of the man for whom the county was named and the self-appointed ruler of all he surveyed. A slender blonde followed in Henry's wake. She was enough to make Ben blink twice.

The woman was a stunner. Smooth, fair skin that somehow managed to look sun-kissed though she wasn't tanned. Laser-bright blue eyes framed by dark lashes and fierce slashes of eyebrows. She was young and long-limbed, with a spill of honey-blond hair so thick and wavy, it made him think of beauty pageant contestants. But this woman wasn't wearing a sash and swimsuit. Or a smile. She wore a stiff navy blue pantsuit and a grimace.

Her posture was straight but rigid. Every inch of her bearing screamed resistance. Ben couldn't help but wonder if it was him, the dingy municipal building or the man she was with she objected to the most. She shot Henry Masters an impatient glance, and Ben felt fairly confident in crossing himself and the building off the list.

"Mr. Masters," he said with a cordial nod.

"Sheriff," the older man said curtly and returned the nod. He placed a hand on the young woman's arm and forced her to take a step forward. "This is my daughter, Marlee. She has recently finished up at Emory Law and will be working for Timber Masters as she awaits

the results from her bar exam. Marlee, this is Ben Kinsella. He's taken over for Bud Walker until the general
election in November."

Ms. Masters extended a hand, her expression making it clear she took no pleasure in meeting him. He
shook her hand briefly, prepared to be no more impressed with her than she was with him. "A pleasure."

"Sheriff," she said, her voice surprisingly husky.

Ben gave his head a subtle shake as he withdrew his
hand from her grasp. He supposed he expected her to
have one of those high, whiny sorority-girl voices, the
type to end every sentence with a question mark. But
no. She'd infused the one-word greeting with enough
smoke to make a man long for a glass of good bourbon.

"We've heard about Clint Young. Tell me what you
know," Henry Masters stated bluntly.

Surprised, Ben shifted his attention back to the older
man and tried to get his sluggish mind to kick into gear.
"What we know?" he repeated.

"Yes," Masters clarified, impatient. "What has your
investigation uncovered?"

Ben took a half step back, wary. Why would Henry
Masters be so upset about Clint Young's death? Sure,
Clint worked for Timber Masters, but Henry could have
called to express his concern. This early-morning office visit seemed a bit over-the-top. "We don't have
much at this juncture," he said, choosing his words
carefully. "Mr. Young's body is being attended by the
coroner at the moment."

"Right, but the scene," Masters pressed, his agitation rising. "What did you find at the scene?"

In the months since Ben had been hired by the Pine Bluff town council to be the interim sheriff of Masters County, he'd thought he had a good gauge on how to handle Henry Masters. Still, he was surprised the man flat-out posed such a question. He had no familial connection to the victim that Ben was aware of. And if being the man's employer was justification enough, Henry might feel free to violate the privacy of three-quarters of the town's residents.

"I'm afraid I can't divulge any information on what is presently an ongoing investigation," he said, repeating the line Julianne had used to dodge the reporters who'd called already. He made a move to stride past them toward the door. "Now, if you'll excuse me, I'll be stepping out for a bit."

Henry gaped at him, as did his daughter. Clearly they were both accustomed to getting what they wanted.

"Wait a minute," the older man sputtered as he wrapped a hand around Ben's arm to stall him.

Ben looked down at the hand, then raised his head, letting the brim of his hat shield his eyes until the last possible moment. Masters released him without another word, but this time, his daughter moved closer.

"Sheriff, we understand you can't give us any of the particulars," she cut in, her voice as mellow and sweet as raw honey dripping from the comb. "It's only... Clint was a neighbor." She let the statement sink in for a moment. "He was my late brother's best friend growing up," she added. Their eyes met, both of them all too aware she could keep dropping these factoids

An Absence of Motive

into the mix if she chose. She might not have lived in Pine Bluff for a while, but she knew the place and its people in a way he never would.

"His mother is…distraught." Something about the way she seemed to settle on that adjective made her father stiffen and the back of Ben's neck prickle. "Word has obviously gotten around town." Her smile was small, sad and no doubt measured to the last millimeter for effectiveness. "People are worried they should lock their doors tonight."

He diverted every ounce of energy he had left in his tank to keeping his expression as unreadable as possible and his pitch uninflected. "People should lock their doors every night. The world is a big, bad place, Ms. Masters."

Her lips pursed slightly, and he would swear he caught a gleam of amusement in those startling blue eyes. "Pine Bluff isn't," she asserted. "Do people need to be worried about a murderer on the loose, Sheriff Kinsella?"

Violent crime was nearly nonexistent in Masters County, but other crimes had taken root. The only reason Ben was there was because Pine Bluff's mayor and the entire county sheriff's department had been swept up in a sting operation run by the federal Drug Enforcement Agency, an operation Ben was familiar with from his time in the agency. His knowledge and experience on that front had been a key factor in securing the job as interim sheriff.

Something about Marlee Masters's demeanor told him she wasn't pleased to be questioning him. She was rigid and annoyed, but she tried to cover it. The blunt questions served up in a syrupy-sweet manner spoke of a woman who wanted to get what she came for and get out. Though it was no hardship to look at her, he found he wished he could give her some answers so she could shed her boring navy pantsuit and run off back to whatever she was doing when Daddy called her home.

Tipping the brim of his cap up so he could meet her frank stare directly, he said, "I wish I had an answer for you. We should have the preliminary report soon."

He cleared his throat to command everyone's full attention as he tore his gaze from hers. Waving a tired hand toward Lori, he directed his comments to Henry Masters when he spoke again. "Deputy Cabrera will call me as soon as the coroner gives us a preliminary." He kept that same hand lifted to stave off any protest the older man might conjure. "I will contact Mrs. Young and you, Mr. Masters, as soon as I have any information, but for now... I've been on duty for nearly thirty-seven hours. Deputy Cabrera will be in charge until I get back."

He pulled his cap down over his eyes again and carefully stepped past Marlee Masters. "It was a pleasure to meet you, Ms. Masters. I am sorry about the circumstances." He inclined his head toward Henry. "Please give Mrs. Masters my best," he said, then made his escape.

He hurried through the door and around the corner to the crumbling concrete parking lot adjacent to the building. The April-morning air was cool but already growing thick with humidity. He opened the door to the

SUV marked with the county sheriff's logo but took a moment before stepping in. By the third deep breath, he felt steady enough, awake enough, to haul himself into the driver's seat and plug the key into the ignition.

He had a feeling something big was happening in his small town. Something big and bad. The kind of thing that wasn't supposed to happen in towns where people didn't lock their doors.

He liked this town. The small, quiet life he was carving out for himself suited him fine, even though it was so different from anywhere he'd ever lived. But when he closed his eyes, he saw the shoes Clint Young had been wearing. Those snow-white kicks. God, how many times had he seen shoes like those on dead bodies? Fresh out of the box. The laces were pristine except for the spatter of blood drying from red to rust.

Blinking away the image, he twisted the key and blew out a gusty breath. Trouble had come to town, and he could only hope the dark shadow of the mess he'd made in Atlanta hadn't followed him here.

Chapter Two

Marlee kept her mouth clamped shut as her father blustered then said his goodbyes. She nodded to Julianne, shot Lori Cabrera a rueful smile then trailed her stomping father out the door.

Things certainly had changed in Pine Bluff.

Including there being a handsome new sheriff in town.

She failed to remember a time when Bud Walker didn't have the sheriff's badge pinned to his barrel chest. She followed her father to the car, dawdling as she looked around the town square. The old courthouse had long been converted to an agricultural museum. The civic facility they'd visited was a low-slung midcentury-modern monstrosity made of pebbled concrete. The U-shaped building housed the sheriff's offices and county jail on one side and the district attorney administrative offices and courtroom on the other. The reception areas on each side were walled with floor-to-ceiling glass, a stylistic choice that reminded Marlee of a fishbowl. She shuddered at the thought of working in such a fishbowl.

Since her mother enjoyed trips to Atlanta to shop and visit, Marlee hadn't come home to Pine Bluff often since she left for college. Now that she was back, she saw the town with fresh eyes. New ornamental lamps dotted the walking path at Parson's Creek. The awning over Brewster's was still bakery-box pink, but this one appeared to be new. It hadn't yet been faded by the sun. She noted the cool weather annuals planted in Lane's Antiques's window boxes. They'd have to be replaced with petunias or geraniums soon, she mused as she reached for the door handle. Summer in southern Georgia was no place for pansies.

The lights flashed on the black Suburban her father drove, startling her from her thoughts. Another change. Since when did her father bother locking his car? When she'd lived in Pine Bluff, she used to leave her ignition key under the floor mat of her Mustang. No one would dare to mess with anything belonging to a Masters. Marlee didn't think she'd ever used the key fob until she moved to Atlanta to go to school.

"Get in already." Her father barked the terse order from the other side of his monstrous SUV.

Marlee bristled but did as she was told. Hoisting herself onto the buttery leather seat, she kept her gaze averted. She couldn't let him see how she truly felt about his orders. Or how much she loathed herself for following them. She loved her father, but she didn't always like him much.

She'd been plotting her escape since the day they buried her brother. Their father had stood stiff as a statue, uncrying, unblinking, as they laid Jeff to rest.

Her mother had been a wreck, crumpling into herself on one of the white wooden folding chairs provided by the funeral home. She'd watched, tears streaming from her eyes, as Jeff's casket was lowered into his grave. But her father showed no signs of grief or weakness, even though he'd only allowed the immediate family at the graveside service.

Now here she was. Summoned home again by news of a death. She needed to get away. Had to figure out a plan to break free from Masters County and everything lying in wait for her. A life she never wanted was closing in around her, and she had to find a way to wriggle off her father's hook.

A mere female, she'd been granted a good deal more leeway than her younger brother. After all, she wasn't the scion. She wasn't supposed to run the family's timber-and-pulp business. She was extraneous, as far as her father was concerned. As long as Jeff was alive and she didn't do anything to make it impossible for her mama to show her face at First Baptist on Sundays, she could do as she pleased. She was brainy enough to graduate at the top of her class and score a spot at Emory University School of Law. Henry assumed once she passed the Georgia bar, she'd come home and serve as her brother's legal counsel and adviser. That was what they'd told him she would do.

Diploma in hand, she'd hunkered down and immersed herself in preparing for the bar exam. But Jeff's death had blown all their plans to smithereens. She'd thought her father wouldn't notice her staying in Atlanta. She'd hoped he'd had his hands full enough with the business and Mama to keep him off her back for a while. But nothing got past Henry Masters.

"Your mother wants you to go with her to visit Eleanor Young this afternoon." It was a command, not an invitation. "I'd appreciate it if you could encourage her to keep her wits about her until after y'all get home."

Marlee opened her mouth to protest but clamped it shut and forced herself to swallow her rebellion. She had to play it cool. Be a Masters.

"Fine," she said tightly.

He cast a sidelong glance at the pantsuit she wore and wrinkled his nose. "You'll want to change into something more…appropriate."

She glanced down at the tailored coordinates she'd chosen so carefully. This was her interview suit. She'd thought it would be her *lucky* interview suit after she had alterations made. She'd had a meeting lined up at one of Atlanta's hottest law firms. Then her father had called to tell her about Clint's death and ordered her to come home.

"This is perfectly appropriate," she said in a quiet voice, trying to keep the rage bubbling inside of her to a low, rolling boil.

"It's unflattering, ill-fitting," her father said bluntly. "What an actor would think an attorney wears." With another sideways glance, he smirked. "You are an attorney, aren't you? You didn't fib about sittin' for the bar exam and all, did you, Miss Marlee?"

His condescending use of what was once a beloved childhood nickname fanned the flame under her anger. Her ears grew hot and prickly. A flush crept up her neck and into her cheeks. She resisted the urge to press her hands to her scalding face. She wouldn't give him the satisfaction.

"I can show you my registration papers when we get back to the house. I brought my diploma with me too, since you couldn't be bothered to come to my graduation."

He dismissed her hurt with a wave of his hand. "I told you your mama wasn't up for the trip."

She disengaged. There was no sense in arguing. The man believed he was the law, both in the family and in the whole county. Dealing with an ego the size of his was akin to running headlong into a brick wall—repeatedly. One she'd been butting up against her whole life. And he and her mother were a pair. For better and for worse. Looking out the window as they cruised through town, she couldn't resist prodding him.

"You don't seem to care much for the new sheriff," she said, striving for casual observation.

"He's fine. I hired him, didn't I?"

She stifled a huff at the defensiveness in his response. Henry Masters considered himself an expert strategist, and he hated any implication he might possibly be ruled by a stray emotion.

"Besides, it doesn't matter if I like him or not. The man has a job to do, and as the head of the town council, it's my responsibility to make sure he does."

Responsibility. Duty. Legacy. Those were three of her father's favorite words. And now... Now he wanted her to do her duty to the Masters family legacy and pay a condolence call to the mother of the boy who was once Jeff's best friend. Her stomach tightened into a knot.

"I need you to go with your mother to represent the family, Marlee. I can't send Carolee alone." He cast a meaningful look in her direction. "Maybe you can ask your mama to help you pick out something to wear. That would make her happy."

He spoke in a low, cajoling tone—the same tenor she'd fallen for repeatedly when she was a child. When a simple request from him could make her strive to do better. But she wasn't a young girl desperate for her daddy's approval anymore. And nothing short of Jeff's resurrection would make her mother happy.

MARLEE PASSED THE afternoon grasping a sweating glass of iced tea and watching her mother and Eleanor Young sit huddled together, clasping hands and crying. She'd been pretty teary herself, but when she pulled a fresh handkerchief from her mother's handbag, she'd spotted a silver flask tucked inside. The sight stirred fresh worry that her mother's emotions might be fueled by something other than pure grief. Marlee just hoped that the friends and neighbors coming to pay call were too focused on Mrs. Young to notice that Carolee Masters was listing ever so slightly to the left.

Townspeople came and went, passing in and out of the Youngs' once-chic, but now truly shabby, parlor in a steady stream. The visitors greeted each other in passing, but no one lingered. They reminded Marlee of relay racers anxious to pass the baton.

Her mother touched a hand-embroidered handkerchief to the corners of her eyes. It came away damp but unmarred by mascara or makeup. Marlee realized with a jolt that sometime in the months since Jeff's death, her mother had morphed her mourning into a kind of performance art.

She studied the two women, the more analytical part of Marlee's brain comparing and contrasting. Eleanor Young was a mess. She alternately sobbed and sniffled. Her face was pale but blotchy from crying. If she'd started the day wearing any kind of cosmetics, they were long gone. Tendrils of curling brown hair escaped the clip worn at the nape of her neck. Marlee had been stunned by the streaks of silver visible at the crown of her hair. Going gray gracefully was simply not done in these parts. Rinker's Drugstore kept Clairol Light Auburn 6R specifically for the county's oldest resident, Miss Louisa Shelby. But Eleanor Young seemed to be flouting convention with at least three inches' growth.

"Excuse me, Mrs. Young?"

The request was spoken in a voice so deep and resonant it sliced through the hum of murmured conversation. Marlee looked up to find Sheriff Ben Kinsella standing on the threshold, wearing a freshly pressed uniform and carrying his broad-brimmed hat in his hands. She took in his height and wide shoulders along with a sharp, short breath. The man was impressive.

He noticed her then and gave a nod of acknowledgment. "Ms. Masters."

Attraction flared hot in the pit of Marlee's stomach, and the sensation made her jostle tea onto her hand. Her cheeks burned as she fumbled for her paper napkin. Had he been this handsome when they were introduced? She must have been too peeved about being hauled down to the station by her father to notice. But how could any woman with breath in her body not notice a man like him?

Dark hair curled close to his head. He was clean-shaven—a fact she appreciated, as it allowed her to map the planes of his face. Tawny skin stretched taut over high cheekbones and a jaw so square he could have been a cartoon hero. But there was nothing flat or two-dimensional about this man. Even standing still in a stuffy parlor, Ben Kinsella personified the word *dynamic*. He appeared to be tightly coiled. Ready to spring into action. Desire snaked through her, moving as stealthily as smoke.

He directed his full attention to the distraught woman on the worn velvet settee. "I'm sorry to interrupt, Mrs. Young, but I'd promised to call as soon as I had news from the coroner," he said, his voice low and sympathetic.

Her mother and Mrs. Young looked up at the same time. They wore matching expressions of apprehensive hope. Marlee had to marvel at the resiliency of the human spirit. What good news could they possibly expect from him? Clint was dead. So was Jeff. The sheriff's presence certainly enhanced the room, but nothing truly good could come from this visit.

"Yes, Sheriff?" Eleanor prompted in a tremulous voice as she started to rise.

"No, no," he said, waving her back into her seat as he strode into the room. "Please, don't get up."

A handful of curious residents had followed him into the Young house. Marlee spotted Trudy Skyler, the woman who ran the local paper, lurking behind Mr. Jensen, the middle school math teacher. But her attention was drawn back to the sheriff.

He stood towering over the settee for a moment, then lowered himself to one knee in order to look Mrs. Young directly in the eye. Something about the gesture tugged Marlee out of her wayward thoughts. Wetting her lips, she leaned forward on her chair, drawn to Ben Kinsella by more than that invisible thread of attraction.

"Mrs. Young, I wanted to come to tell you I've spoken to the coroner." Marlee saw his gaze shift to her mother and back. "He is not going to refer the case to the medical examiner's office. Your son's body will be released immediately and the case closed."

Someone behind the sheriff gasped, but Marlee couldn't see who it was. She only heard a woman whisper, "I told you. It's just like Carolee's boy."

Sheriff Kinsella continued, "Mel Schuler asked me to assure you he'd take care of Clint. He said if you would go down to the funeral home in the morning, he'd like to go over all the arrangements with you."

The moment Sheriff Kinsella spoke her son's name, Eleanor Young broke down in big, gulping sobs and collapsed against Marlee's mother, hardly noticing Carolee Masters was better equipped to accept comfort than to dole it out.

"I am truly sorry for your loss, Mrs. Young," he concluded, his voice lower and gravelly.

Marlee watched in helpless horror as her own mother, having far more experience in playing the part of the bereaved, offered the sheriff a limp hand to shake. "Thank you so much for taking the time to come yourself, Sheriff. I'm sure Eleanor appreciates all your efforts."

"It's the least I could do, ma'am," he replied. "I truly am sorry."

"Thank you," Carolee said, bowing her head as she extracted her hand. "So kind of you to say. You're new to our town, Sheriff. Do come to the house one night for supper," she instructed with a faint upward tilt of her lips. "We'd be pleased to have you."

Marlee rose as the sheriff did, her fascinated stare fixed on her mother. Apparently, it wasn't possible to drown a lifetime of grace and poise in vodka. Glancing over the sheriff's shoulder, she was relieved to note the soul-shaking sobs emanating from the parlor had driven the gossips from the foyer. The implication of what he'd said, of the coroner's ruling on Clint's death, weighed heavy on her heart. She needed to be certain she understood him correctly.

"Sheriff," she called as he pivoted to leave. "Does this mean—"

She pressed a hand to her neck, hoping to calm her own racing pulse. Grabbing his arm, she propelled him away from the weeping women on the couch and toward the now-empty foyer. When they stopped near the Youngs' front door, she couldn't quite bring herself to relinquish her hold on his solid bicep. The man felt strong. Sturdy. Secure. All the things she hadn't felt since her brother died.

Marlee looked up to find him gazing down at her searchingly, his brown eyes dark with sympathy. He covered her hand with his, and her pulse leaped. She looked into his eyes, wondering if he even realized he'd done it. Surely, the gesture was meant to comfort and nothing more. She couldn't stand there and let a total stranger hold her hand, no matter how good it felt. Could he feel how fast her heart was beating?

"Ms. Masters? Can I help you?"

She forced herself to slide her hand from his grasp. Marlee didn't want sympathy. She wanted to get out of there. More than anything, she wanted to be anywhere other than where she was, about to ask what she had to ask. Drawing a shaky breath, she forced the question out in a rush.

"Does this mean Mr. Schuler believes Clint took his own life?"

Her gaze dropped to the badge affixed to Ben Kinsella's uniform tunic as he drew in a deep breath, then reluctantly let it go. "It means we could find no evidence to make us think anyone other than the victim was involved in the shooting."

His careful phrasing snagged her interest. Her eyes widened with the dawning realization the new sheriff had found something about Clint's death puzzling. "'No evidence,'" she repeated. Sheriff Walker had said something similar when he'd talked to her family about Jeff.

"Yes, ma'am," he confirmed.

His use of the word *ma'am* made Marlee flinch, but she refrained from saying anything about it. After all, she was the daughter of the town's most prominent citizen. She'd been called "miss" and "ma'am" and treated with deference her entire life. Even if she hadn't done a thing to deserve it.

Sheriff Kinsella looked as itchy and uncomfortable as she felt, but still he stayed, waiting for her to speak her piece with infinite patience.

She averted her gaze to the fine mesh of the screen door. One push and the lucky man would be free to go. Would she ever be? Drawing a shaky breath, she fell back on the lessons learned in a lifetime of training.

"Thank you for coming by, Sheriff. Shall I pass the message along to my father?"

He hesitated, and she saw his cheeks darken with a flush. "Thank you, but no," he said, donning his hat with a touch too much force, then adjusting the brim to ride low over his eyes. "I've already spoken to him."

The screen door slapped against the old wood casing, punctuating their conversation. Marlee's estimation of the new sheriff in town clicked up a couple notches. The man was clearly tuned in to who ruled the roost in Masters County.

"Why, yes, of course you have," she said to his retreating back, her fingers tangling in the slim gold chain she wore at her throat as she watched the handsome man stride away from the house. With a tired sigh, she stepped back and closed the heavy front door. The grieving Mrs. Young would not be receiving any more callers.

Chapter Three

"It wouldn't kill Patti Cummings to go a week or two between visits to the Curl Up and Dye," a woman behind him whispered loudly. "I swear, I can hear her hair calling out for a deep conditioning all the way across the room."

"Now, Susie," another woman's voice cautioned, suppressing laughter.

"I'm only sayin' the bleach is turnin' her hair to straw."

Ben tuned out, mentally filing the conversation under "idle gossip" in his mind. He eyed the woman currently condoling with Mrs. Young and cringed internally. The Susie lady hadn't been entirely wrong in her assessment. Patti Cummings had hair the color and presumed texture of sun-bleached wheat.

Biting back the urge to chuckle, he attempted to blend into the back wall of the funeral parlor's viewing room. Of course, he knew trying not to stand out in Pine Bluff was a silly notion. Sure, there were plenty of people of color in the area. They'd tried to welcome him to their churches and socials. But it was hard for folks to get past the sheriff's badge on his uniform shirt. His profession, coupled with the fact that he was city born and raised, made people uncomfortable. Particularly here, where the sweeps made by federal law enforcement had impacted so many families.

Scanning the room, he did his best to put names with the faces he recognized. The town was small, but he'd only lived there for a few months. He wished he'd asked Lori to come to the visitation. She'd grown up in town and could give him the lowdown.

"Coffee, boss?"

Ben jerked, then gaped at his deputy, wondering— not for the first time—if she was some kind of mind reader.

Lori winced. "Sorry, I thought you heard me say your name."

She pointed toward the lobby. "Coffee? I have to warn you, it's not as good as Julianne's, but it's a sight better than the sludge you brew."

Ben smirked. "Maybe in a minute." He cocked his head to indicate that he was listening to the people around him. "I was thinking I should have asked you to come tonight."

"No need to ask," Lori said, scanning the room. "I'd have been here anyway."

Ben stared at her dumbly for a moment, trying to remember if he'd ever bothered to ask if she was acquainted with the deceased. "Did you know—"

She shook her head, cutting him off. "No. I mean, not well. One of his cousins on his mama's side was in my class. I was a couple years ahead of them." She nodded to a knot of people who bore a vague resemblance to the woman standing in front of the casket. "Doesn't take much to make a connection in these parts."

"You were coming anyway," he concluded.

"Everyone will," she corrected with quiet certainty. "The only people who don't show up for a visitation here are the ones who don't give a damn about what anyone says about them. Reputation is currency in a small town. There's a pecking order, and believe me, attendance is taken."

He pressed his lips together then gave Lori a grateful nudge with his elbow. "Noted."

He spotted some familiar faces. Camille Brewster from the bakery visited with a small cluster of women as they inched forward. Chet Rinker, the pharmacist, stood solemn-faced and stared in a trance at the wooden cross suspended behind the casket at the front of the room. An older woman with bright red hair stood behind him, leaning heavily on her walker but steadfastly refusing all offers of assistance, cups of water and vacated chairs. He speculated she might be *the* Miss Louisa Shelby. People loved to tell tales about the town's oldest and most colorful resident.

"Where's Clint Young's father?"

"Ran off with his secretary about ten years ago," Lori supplied quietly.

"Secretary?"

"He was Henry Masters's right-hand man at Timber Masters until he got bit by the love bug," she reported. "About the time Clint would have been starting junior high, I guess." She gave her head a sad shake and searched the crowd. "I don't think he's here. They moved off somewhere. Tupelo? Tuscaloosa? Some city with a *T*." She shrugged. "Anyhow, it was big gossip for a long time. Still is."

"Really? Even that long ago," he commented, shooting her a skeptical look.

"Gossip moves fast, but people's memories are long." She gave him a smirk. "This isn't the city. Not a lot happens here, so when something does, people tend to hang on to it."

There was a rustling commotion at the back of the room, and the line of mourners shifted, moving to one side of the aisle or the other. Henry Masters made his way into the room, pausing to exchange nods, handshakes, shoulder squeezes and cheek kisses with nearly every man or woman he passed. His wife and daughter followed in his wake but left the glad-handing to him. The women doled out smiles and pats on the arm here and there, but it was clear Henry was the man to be hailed.

When Henry clasped both of Eleanor Young's hands between his and bent his head close to speak to her, Ben remembered something he'd overheard at the Youngs' house. "Do they have a son?"

He felt Lori stiffen beside him and tore his attention from the blonde on the other side of the room to look at her. "What?"

"The Masters," he clarified. "Do they have a son?"

She gaped at him, but Ben simply waited for an answer. Patience was often the most effective tool in getting people to talk.

"Yes. Jeff. His name was Jeff." She cleared her throat, then spoke in a quiet, but infinitely steadier, manner. "Jeff Masters. Why do you ask?"

"Was?" He leaned forward, inviting her to continue.

Lori swallowed hard and said only, "He passed away less than a year ago."

Ben felt an instant stab of remorse. "You knew him."

She huffed a laugh. "I'm sure it's strange to you because you're new here and all, but we all know each other. Everyone." She looked up, meeting his gaze directly. "Some of us better than others, but we all 'know' each other," she said, using air quotes to emphasize the difference in degrees of knowledge.

Something about the deflection pinged his radar. "How well did you know Jeff Masters?" Suddenly, he realized he was asking the wrong question. "Wait. How did Jeff Masters die?"

Lori pressed her lips together and shook her head. He caught the shimmer of unshed tears in her eyes, then she pivoted on her heel and pushed past the guests lingering at the back of the room to get to the reception area. Torn between going after her to press for answers and the uneasy feeling in his gut, he hesitated. The room hummed around him. Quiet conversation charged with a buzz of tension. He looked to the front and found Henry Masters had escorted the old woman with the walker past the people in line and delivered her to Eleanor Young.

He scanned the room and spotted Carolee Masters seated in the front row. As always, she was immaculately dressed in a navy blue suit with black piping. Her slender ankles were crossed and tucked neatly beneath her seat. She sat still and straight, her face pointed toward the casket. Unmoving.

The hairs on his arms prickled as he sought Marlee Masters. Something told him she'd stick close to her mother. He wasn't wrong.

She stood near the end of the front row, her bearing erect and alert. Protective. Clearly ready to run interference for her mother, if the need arose. The air in his lungs grew too full and hot for him to hold. He exhaled in a long gust as he took her in. There was nothing provocative or the least bit suggestive in the styling of the black dress she wore, but the fabric draped and clung to her curves. She wore the same killer shoes she'd had on when she accompanied her father to town hall, but they were miles more lethal paired with the dress rather than the pantsuit.

When he lifted his head, he found her staring back at him, her jaw tight and tilted at a defensive angle.

A sizzle of awareness traveled up his spine, but Marlee Masters didn't back down.

Aware his stare would be considered rude, he inclined his head, then looked away.

A group of young women approached Marlee with a hushed glee wholly inappropriate in the setting. She looked decidedly uncomfortable as they closed around her, chattering and gushing over her, completely oblivious to the fact they were in a funeral home.

"Killed himself, they say," an older man seated in one of the back rows said, his volume making up for what was clearly his own hearing loss.

"I heard he was runnin' with a bad crowd, but…"

The last part of the snippet dangled tantalizingly, but Ben had no idea who gave voice to the speculation. There were at least a dozen women in his vicinity.

"I took a seven-layer salad," a woman to his right said to the woman sitting next to her. The two of them waved paper fans attached to oversize Popsicle sticks in the general direction of their faces. "It's so hard to know what to do. I couldn't just throw together a tater-tot casserole," the first woman complained, pausing midwave to cast a glance at her friend. She sniffed her disdain. "Women like Eleanor and Carolee don't eat carbohydrates. They aren't normal people."

"Lord, no," her friend concurred. "Everyone knows Carolee Masters is perpetually on a liquid diet."

The two women snickered and resumed their desultory fanning. For the first time, Ben noticed how warm the room had become. A rivulet of sweat ran down his spine as he checked the door. The crush of people kept coming.

He wasn't going to be able to make heads or tails out of any of the things he overheard. He'd unwittingly tripped headfirst into a sticky spiderweb of small-town connections. But he had to figure out where he'd gone wrong. He needed his deputy to provide some context. Resolved, he headed toward the lobby, hoping she hadn't decided to leave.

She sat in a small alcove, perched on the edge of a velvet settee looking shell-shocked. In one hand she clutched a napkin with two chocolate chip cookies, and in the other, a bottle of water perspiring only slightly more than he was.

He rubbed the back of his neck. He'd never seen his deputy looking so vulnerable, and he had to say, the look didn't suit her. "How are you doing?"

She peered up at him, then past him. The corners of her mouth tilted up as she nodded to the procession of people waiting to pay their respects. "There's my family."

He spotted a cluster of people who matched Lori's tawny coloring at the tail end of the line. The youngest of the children appeared to be no older than ten. "Oh, wow." Then, realizing his reaction probably wasn't the correct one, he gave a self-effacing laugh. "Sorry, uh, big family."

"I'm the oldest of seven," she said with a low nod. She wrinkled her nose, but a devilish light sparked in her dark eyes. "Cath-o-lics," she said in a stage whisper. "What can you do?"

Ben chuckled. For the first time, it occurred to him Lori was nearly as much of an outsider in this town as he was. The only difference was, she'd been born here.

He nodded to the empty spot beside her. "May I?"

She scooted to the side to allow him more room. "Sure."

"I didn't mean to upset you. I guess I'm figuring out what to ask and what not to ask."

"This town is full of quicksand." He waited while she took a deep pull on the water bottle. His patience was rewarded. "I was seeing Jeff Masters when he died," she said, low and confidential.

"Was it a secret?"

She shook her head, and her lips curved downward. "No, not a secret, but there were plenty of people who didn't approve."

"Like who?"

She snorted a laugh. "His parents, mine, anyone who didn't think the crown prince of Pine Bluff should be spending time with me," she said, waving the water bottle in an all-encompassing circle.

"Why not?"

"Because I'm not white," she said bluntly. He sputtered a weak protest, but she plowed ahead. "Oh, I'd be good enough for some people but not for Jeff Masters."

"I see."

They lapsed into silence for a minute. Ben watched as people slipped out of the room. A few sidled closer to the exit as they greeted newcomers, no doubt hoping they could sneak out without anyone taking note.

"He killed himself," she said softly. He jerked his head around to look at her, but she kept her eyes fixed on the water bottle in her hands. She picked at the loose edge of the label with her thumbnail.

"I'm sorry."

"We hadn't been together long. And no, I don't know why." Her words were spoken thoughtfully, as though she was shifting through memories in her mind. She gave a short laugh, then took a sip of her water. Straightening her shoulders, she looked him directly in the eye. "I guess I fooled myself into believing we were more than we were. He certainly didn't give me a second thought in the end."

"I am sorry," he repeated, enunciating each word in the hopes his sincerity might ring through.

"Anyway…" She studied the cookies with disinterest. "I'm trying to move on, but now Clint." She sighed. "They say something about how one suicide can lead to others, don't they?"

"There are theories, I suppose," he said carefully.

She bit the cookie in half, then chewed. "It's weird, though. Clint and Jeff used to be friends. They fell out years ago. I don't have any answers for why," she added with a preemptive glance at him. "But I can't imagine Clint being so torn up over Jeff he'd do the same thing."

"Maybe they were unrelated," he said gently.

Lori shook her head, her sadness palpable. "Maybe," she murmured, but she sounded unconvinced.

He wanted to press her to explain, but a pair of shiny, expensive-looking black high heels appeared in front of him. He fixated on them for a moment, then allowed himself the luxury of savoring every inch of Marlee Masters's long, lithe frame as he lifted his head.

"I'm sorry to interrupt," she said. The agitation in her posture clearly indicated the woman didn't have a sorry bone in her body. She wanted their attention, and she wanted it now. Something about her demeanor made him want to shut her down, but then she shifted her focus to Lori, and her expression softened.

"Hey, Lori." She paired the casual greeting with a brief flutter of her hand. "Can you help me?"

Lori met the other woman's gaze, surprise written all over her face. "Um, sure."

Marlee darted a quick glance at him, then shrugged.

"I guess you can see this too." She thrust out her phone, and Ben watched as his deputy carefully took it from her.

Lori cradled the device in both hands. He didn't blame her for the extra caution. Replacing that particular model could eat up a mere mortal's entire paycheck—before taxes. Which, he supposed, made sense. Marlee Masters seemed the type to be accustomed to having the latest and greatest.

He tipped his head to the side as he looked at the blank screen. "What's going on?"

"Oh, sorry. Here." She plucked the phone from Lori's hands and unlocked the screen by flashing a megawatt grin at the camera. The moment it sprang to life, she ditched the beauty queen routine and placed the phone back in Lori's hands. "Open the message app."

Lori did, and Ben leaned close enough to see a string of text conversations appear. There were a couple labeled "Dad," one with "Mom" and a whole string of others showing only ten-digit phone numbers rather than contact information.

Lori opened the first of the unlabeled texts. It read simply, Welcome home.

Lori tapped back to the list screen, her expression tightening. "I take it you don't know who this was from?"

Marlee shook her head. "No."

The next message read, Lookin good marlee.

His deputy snorted and clicked off the second message, mumbling, "Too busy for capitalization or punctuation, I see. I guess we can narrow it down to someone who flunked English in school."

Marlee laughed, but the sound was mirthless.

Ben peered over Lori's shoulder. The third and fourth messages were along the same vein. One, a brief approval of the dress she'd worn to visit Eleanor Young; the other, unsolicited commentary on whether she should be eating whatever it was she had been carrying in a Brewster's Bakery box.

"Nunya, you jerk," Lori muttered as she clicked back to the list of messages.

She started to open the next text, but Ben stopped her with a hand on her wrist. "Wait."

Both women swung startled gazes in his direction. "What?" Lori asked, suddenly on high alert.

"They get worse," Marlee said, frustration making her voice low and tight.

"They're all from different numbers," he said, pointing to the list on the phone. "Have you tried to call any of these numbers?"

At last, he felt the full force of Marlee's blue-flame eyes on him. "Yes. They all go to a recording saying the person is unavailable."

Rubbing his chin, Ben shook his head. "Burner phones or some kind of automated thing?" he puzzled aloud.

"No clue. Read the last one. It came while I was in there," she informed them, nodding toward the viewing parlor.

Ben tore his gaze from Marlee's troubled expression, his gut tightening with dread as Lori scrolled to the most recent text and opened it.

Can't wait to see more of you.

He looked up and found Marlee Masters staring directly into his eyes, and the only words that popped into his mind were *Me too.*

GOD, SHE HADN'T wanted to get the hot sheriff involved in this, but the last message had come through minutes ago, and it freaked her out. She'd abandoned her mother long enough to give official condolences to Mrs. Young and settle Miss Louisa Shelby into one of the chairs in the front row, walker close at hand. Her father was still working the room, so she'd picked up her purse and clutched it close as she claimed the chair next to her mother.

She'd felt the vibration indicating an incoming message. Murmuring a weak cover story about needing a tissue, she'd opened her bag and took out her phone. But what had once been a chastisable offense in her mother's eyes hadn't mattered. Carolee Masters's once all-seeing gaze was completely glazed over.

Now, Sheriff Kinsella was looking at her, and she couldn't look away. His dark eyes burned with intensity as he nudged Lori Cabrera with his elbow and extended his hand, broad palm up. "May I?"

She eyeballed him, wondering what his angle might be. After all, he'd been reading along with them the whole time. But now, he was asking permission. Despite what most people thought of her, Marlee was far more accustomed to being told what to do. The question was a formality, but he was giving her the power to say yes or no. The very fact that he gave her a choice made her want to give him anything he wanted.

"Of course."

He took the phone from Lori and began opening and closing the text messages with a detached efficiency she found herself envying. She'd been tempted to delete the messages when they first started, but the better judgment gleaned in three years of law school tempered the impulse. Evidence. Her gut told her these creepy texts from some rando might one day be evidence, so she kept them.

"Do you mind if I write these numbers down?" The sheriff pulled a small notepad and a pen from his shirt pocket.

"Knock yourself out," she said.

"We'll check them out," Lori promised.

Marlee refocused her attention on the younger woman. She hadn't known Lori growing up. They had years and multiple layers of social strata between them, but her brother had dated her. Maybe even spent his last months falling in love with her. From what she'd seen in the days surrounding Jeff's funeral, Lori had loved him too.

"How are you doing?" Marlee kept her voice quiet and gentle.

The other woman raised a shoulder and let it fall. "I'm okay." She glanced beyond Marlee's shoulder, her gaze straying to her family. "Most days."

"But not today," Marlee answered with gentle understanding.

"Exactly."

Marlee watched as Ben Kinsella noted every phone number, as well as the date and time received, in his notebook. There likely wasn't much he could do with the information in terms of tracing the messages, but having someone else see them, having the information listed somewhere other than in her phone, made her feel more secure.

He finished, closing the notebook and giving the cover a little tap. Despite her father's bluster the other day, she trusted this man. Whether she approved of Ben Kinsella's method or management, Henry obviously did.

"Thank you," she said. "I…" She blew out a breath, and her shoulders relaxed for the first time in days. "I needed to show someone." She gave a self-deprecating wince. "See if someone else thought it was creepy or if I'm crazy."

"You're not crazy," Lori said to her without a beat of hesitation. She gestured to the phone Marlee clutched in her hand. "Super creepy."

The succinct assessment startled a laugh from her. "Thank you."

"If you get any other messages, would you contact me?" Sheriff Kinsella pulled a business card from the same breast pocket where he'd kept the notebook.

She took it, noting the heavy card stock retained the warmth of his body. "Yes. Thank you."

Marlee turned to leave them, but his deep voice stopped her in her tracks. "Ms. Masters?"

"Yes?"

"How long do you plan to stay in Pine Bluff?"

The question cut to the quick, but she couldn't let it show. She wouldn't let any of them see how desperate she was to leave. Her father had her trapped here for the moment, but she'd find a way out. She had to if she wanted any kind of life of her own. But for now, she needed to keep a cool head and not fight the ties that bound her there. Because everyone knew the harder you fought to free yourself, the tighter a snare became.

"Indefinitely," she said, lifting her arms out, presenting herself to them. "I'm home. Take care, Lori." She backed off a step and raised a hand in farewell. She was done with this conversation. "Thanks, Sheriff. I appreciate y'all."

Chapter Four

Home from the visitation, Marlee avoided the cross fire of her parents' lame attempts at conversation by escaping to her room. The door closed tightly behind her, she planted both hands flat on the tall four-poster bed for balance as she stepped out of the torturous high heels. Moaning her relief, she curled her toes into the plush pile of the rug beside the bed and reached for the zip on her dress.

Black fabric pooled on the floor, and she sighed as the cool air flowing from the vents breezed over her heated skin. She unhooked her bra as she moved to the cherrywood bureau. In one practiced motion, she let it fall into the open drawer, then she pulled on the first T-shirt she found.

It was one of Jeff's. She'd rescued a bunch from his room when her mother was in the midst of a grief-fueled purge. The hem fell halfway down her thighs, even though her brother had been only an inch taller. The Greek letters screen-printed onto the fabric were still stiff and uncracked from washing. A reminder of how young Jeff had been when he died.

She ran her fingers along the collar of the shirt, stretching the fabric away from her throat. She shook her arms out and gave her shoulders a couple rolls to loosen her tense muscles as she approached the bed. The leather clutch she'd carried to the visitation lay atop the rumpled coverlet. She opened it and removed the lipstick, card case and her phone. She tossed the lipstick into the depths of the larger handbag parked beside the bed, removed her identification and debit cards from the small leather case and placed them on the nightstand before connecting her phone to its charger.

The screen woke but showed no new notifications. She dropped down onto the bed, drawing one leg up under her as she settled in to relisten to the voice mail she'd received a mere hour after her father called to summon her home. Pressing the play button was the technological equivalent to testing a bruise, but she couldn't help herself. She tapped the screen, and the speaker hummed to life.

"Marlee, hello. I'm sorry we keep missing each other." Jared Baker, senior partner at one of Atlanta's hottest firms, had the kind of mellow baritone voice both women and juries loved. But she'd been impervious to him. All she'd wanted was a job in Atlanta. "I received your message about a family emergency, and I understand completely. I was going to have to cancel our appointment anyway. I, uh, I'm sorry to tell you my partner and I have decided not to take a new associate at this time. I'm sorry to disappoint you, but I wish you the best in your future endeavors. Please give my best to your family."

Her family.

The Masters name strikes another blow against freedom, Marlee thought, her stomach souring.

She blew out a breath that ruffled her hair, then let her head fall back. Staring up at the ceiling, she drew a couple deep breaths to center herself. Here she was, back in her childhood bedroom, doing her father's bidding. Squinting at what appeared to be a small brown water mark on the ceiling above her bed, she concentrated on resuming the natural flow of her breathing as she forced her racing mind to slow.

She straightened her neck and raised her hands over her head with her fingers laced together, stretching every muscle as long as she could make them. When she let go, she fell back across the bed, snatching her phone up as she flopped.

A trickle of trepidation rippled through her as she saw she had an unread text message awaiting her. More than the unsolicited commentary on her daily activities, she truly resented the creep for making her not want to look at her phone. Setting her jaw, she jabbed at the icon to open her message queue. The breath she'd been holding rushed from her lungs when she saw the text was a terse reminder from her father to be at Timber Masters offices no later than eight the next morning.

She wasn't likely to forget.

Marlee resented being called home from Atlanta. Sure, he'd only agreed to pay her rent until she'd sat for the bar exam, but she had hoped she could stretch things out long enough for her to land a job and get a paycheck or two into her account. She promised herself this layover in Pine Bluff would be nothing but a speed bump. As soon as she could, she was getting out of town.

Her phone buzzed and she automatically lifted her hand to see the screen. Another unknown ten-digit number. Feeling more confident having shared them with the sheriff and Lori, she tapped to open the message.

Nobody likes a tattletail

A chill ran down her spine as she sat up straight once more. This time, she couldn't find even a modicum of comfort in the sender's grammatical errors or misspellings. A second later, a different phone number appeared.

I like this outfit even better then the dress you wore earlier

The message came across loud and clear. Whoever it was, they were watching her. All the time. She growled her annoyance at both the arrogance and the grammatical offenses, but the sound tangled in her throat and morphed into a groan when her phone buzzed again.

You should show more skin marlee you have nice legs

Whipping her head around, she checked the window. The blinds were open. Cursing under her breath, she slid off the corner of the bed, scurried to the wall and slid over to the window. Her heart hammered as she twisted the rod to close the slats.

Once she felt certain she couldn't be seen, she yanked the sheer curtains from their decorative holders and closed them over the entire window. Feeling more secure with a few extra millimeters of nylon between her and her peeper, she gripped her phone tightly, willing her hand to stop shaking.

Her gaze caught on the clutch she'd abandoned on the bed. Forcing herself not to lunge for it, she walked over to the bag and extracted the business card Ben Kinsella had given her. A mobile number was listed beneath the office phone and fax.

She dialed, allowing her mind to ruminate on the necessity of a fax number these days as she poked at the screen. Closing her eyes, she pressed the phone to her ear and concentrated on faking a normal breathing pattern until her brain got the message all was well. And all *was* well. Her parents' house had a state-of-the-art security system. She was safe. Whoever was doing this was nothing more than a creep—

"Kinsella."

The deep, masculine bark startled her out of the circular pattern of her thoughts. She blurted the first thing that sprang to mind. "He's watching me."

There was a beat of silence on the other end of the line. She cringed, squeezing her eyes shut tight in mortification as a rush of blood set her cheeks and ears afire. "I mean, I was changing clothes—"

"Are you home alone?" he broke in, brusquely efficient.

"What? No. My parents are here," she stammered. "I'm safe. A bit…freaked. He texted me."

"He?"

"I assume it's a he," she said haltingly. "I guess, maybe… I'm not sure. Maybe I shouldn't assume, but the things he says are things a perverted guy would say."

"What did he say?"

"He called me a tattletale, said that he preferred what I'm wearing now to the dress I wore to the visitation. He also remarked about my nice legs."

There was a pause, then a small cough as the sheriff cleared his throat. "This is probably going to sound out of line, but I don't have the first idea how else to ask… What are you wearing?"

"A T-shirt," she admitted. "One of my brother's old shirts."

"A men's T-shirt," he repeated, and Marlee got the vague impression he was making another note in his notebook. "And…?" Another awkward moment hung between them, then he exhaled a soft, "Ah."

"Yeah."

"Well, uh…" His words stumbled to a halt.

"My blinds were open," she confessed in a rush. "I didn't think to close them. I came in and wanted to get out of my dress and shoes."

"And then you received the text," he said, a husky edge in his voice.

"Three texts, actually," she clarified. "First, he called me a tattletale. Then the one about the dress and the other about my legs." She sat down on the edge of the bed with a huff, then dropped her head into her hand. "Different phone numbers."

"Answers my next question."

"I figured."

"Do you feel safe? Do you want me to call your father and let him in on what's happening?"

Her head jerked up. "No. No. Do not tell my father," she ordered.

"But, Marlee—"

"I'm serious. I only wanted to tell you what was happening in case I ever felt…not safe. Come to think of it, I never meant to tell you. I was telling Lori. If I wanted to tell my father, I would have gone to him. Don't call my father."

"I won't."

She snorted softly. "Sure you won't."

"I said I wouldn't and I won't." His annoyance sliced off all the softer notes of his earlier agreement.

"Please." She scoffed. "No one keeps anything from Henry Masters. Not in this town."

"You told us in confidence. We will keep your confidence."

She gave a bitter laugh. "I'm going to assume you're so new here you haven't even unpacked, but fine. I guess I have no choice but to believe you."

"If you didn't want to take the chance of your father finding out, why did you tell Lori?"

Pressing her hand to her throat, she let her head fall back. "I," she started, stopped, then figured she had nothing to lose at this point. "I wanted to go on record, I guess. In case—" Clamping her mouth shut, she gave a frustrated squeak of irritation. "Good night, Sheriff."

She ended the call.

Staring at the wallpaper she'd added to the phone's

home screen, she swallowed hard. Her brother's smiling face shone up at her, the blue eyes they'd both inherited from their father glowing with amusement. She'd snapped the photo the last time she'd seen him. It had been one of her rare weekends home in Pine Bluff. They'd ditched the house after an excruciating Sunday supper. He'd begged her to hang out with him for a while and she gave in, but only grudgingly.

Regret twisted in her gut, radiating pangs of remorse. Her heart squeezed. She'd resented a couple hours spent with her brother, and weeks later he was dead. Thank God she'd given in. Thank Heaven above she'd climbed into his truck and let him drive her out to their place on Sawtooth Lake.

There, they'd sat on the dock while they daydreamed of a life out from under their father's thumb.

Less than three months later, her brother had been found in the lake house with a bullet in his brain and a gun in his hand.

Ever since the day she'd received that awful phone call, Marlee was aware her time would come. But she'd find a way to face the forces her brother couldn't handle. She didn't have time to be intimidated by some coward who got his jollies sending anonymous messages. And someday, she was going to face her father and tell him she had no intention of staying to help run the family business.

She was going rogue—as she and Jeff had dreamed.

Chapter Five

Ben gripped his phone long after Marlee Masters ended the call. He told himself to stop thinking about how she'd look wearing only a men's T-shirt. Told himself over and over again. But he failed miserably. The image was in his mind now, and there was no shaking it.

He glanced at the plain white undershirt he'd stripped down to upon arriving back at the house he was renting. The place was on the small side but tidy. And furnished. Only two blocks from the town hall and his office. There were days when he felt utterly ridiculous making the one-minute drive to park in the space designated for the sheriff's vehicle, but he couldn't waste time jogging home to get his car in the event of an actual emergency.

He imagined Marlee Masters jogging down his street wearing only a T-shirt similar to the one he wore and her underwear. Blue underwear. Light blue. Bikini cut? Yeah, bikini. Cut to cling to the curve of her hip and colored to match her piercing eyes.

His phone rang again, and he jumped. Heat prickling his neck and cheeks, he checked the display, half-afraid the lovely Ms. Masters might have sensed he was thinking about her in a salacious manner. Thankfully, it was his deputy calling.

"Hey, Lori. You going on shift early?"

"Yeah, I sent Mike on home. He's still pretty shaky," she reported.

"No problem." He cleared his throat, hesitant to bring up the personal stuff she'd been wrestling with at the funeral home but figuring it was better to climb on the elephant in the room and try to ride it out. Emotions were running high all over town. This was another reminder that he wasn't in Atlanta anymore. "And, uh, how are you holding up?"

To his relief, she laughed. "Boy, you suck at this," she teased.

"I do not," he replied, offended. "I'm not used to, uh…" He shrugged, then remembered she couldn't see him. "You know."

She gave another chuckle. "People having feelings? Or, rather, seeing other people's feelings out there on display for the whole town to see?"

He ducked his head. She was dead-on. She also didn't realize how lucky she was to grow up in a place where people actually placed value on feelings, no matter how inconvenient they were.

"Sorry, boss. It won't happen again."

"Don't say you're sorry," he snapped, too on edge to get a good read on his own emotional barometer to control his tone. "You didn't do anything wrong."

"It was pretty unprofessional of me to spill all over you," she began.

He cut off any additional apologies. "It was pretty human of you. And it's not like you were on duty."

She snorted. "I'm sure every time one of your busts went south, you and your old DEA buddies huddled up and had a sharing circle."

"No," he admitted with a chuckle. "But that might also give you some decent insight into how a former agent ends up the sheriff in a rural county." He hesitated for only a moment, then swiped one of the agency shrink's favorite lines. "It's no crime to want some peace in your life."

"I know," she answered softly. "I guess we're all shook up."

"Totally understandable," he said gruffly. "It's natural to think about it, Lori, but make sure you don't dwell. Get me?"

"Yeah. My *abuela* used to tell me not to borrow trouble from tomorrow. There will be plenty to go around when it gets here."

"Your *abuela* was right."

Lori cleared her throat, then slipped back into the brisk, no-nonsense manner he'd grown accustomed to since coming to Pine Bluff. "All is well here, Sheriff. Get some rest. We'll see you in the morning."

"Thanks, Deputy. See you then."

Ben ended the call and sat staring at the television screen without registering what was happening on the cold-case show he'd been watching when his phone rang the first time. Warmth unfurled in his gut. People were starting to trust him here. At least, one was.

The conversations he'd shared with Lori were the

easiest they'd exchanged since the day he walked into the Pine Bluff municipal building. He didn't blame her for being wary of him. Aside from being an outsider, he was also a city guy, and a former federal agent. In these parts, those were the kinds of strikes a guy didn't get a chance to swing at often. The realization made him feel all sorts of warm fuzzies he'd never admit to having.

People had warned him when he took the job. Everyone from the resident agent in charge of his old division to Henry Masters himself had told him he'd have a hard time settling in and an even tougher row to hoe if he wanted to actually belong in his new hometown. Locals were still rattled by the drug busts that exposed the seedy underbellies of several bucolic Georgia towns. But the life of a social outcast was something he could deal with if he had to. A life outside of law enforcement was not on the table.

Tossing his phone aside, he reached for the bottle of beer on the coffee table and took a swig, grimacing as the now-warmish brew flowed past his lips. He cradled the bottle between his palms, laced his fingers together and let his head fall back against the sofa cushion. The ceilings in his cozy house were tongue-and-groove knotty pine. To his surprise, it took him only two nights in this new exile to discover he loved looking at them.

Those ceilings provided endless games of connect-the-knots. Some nights, he assigned the spots of burled wood key points in the cases he'd left open when he'd opted out. Others, he traced and retraced his steps through the maze of deals and double crosses ultimately culminating in his resignation. On the darkest nights, he luxuriated in torturous games of "what if," starting with the large black hole of a knot in the corner of the ceiling, and let the twists and turns of his life lead him from one impossible spot to another until the game ended with his childhood best friend, Andre, emptying a good portion of his bumped-up AR-15 into the agents rushing the room where they'd stood. Though he lived to rue his decision for a whole host of reasons, Ben had had no choice but to take his oldest friend down.

A blown cover and the death of the man he'd once loved as a brother would have been reason enough to move on. The bounty placed on his head by the leader of the SEATL—the notorious southeast Atlanta gang whose business he'd been infiltrating—helped move his decision process along.

Ivan Jones was a white kid born in East Point, Georgia. A maniac with an ego the size of all of Atlanta. In order to survive, he'd spent most of his life telling everyone who'd listen that his family was connected to the Russian mafia. His parents were actually penniless Serbian refugees, but the truth didn't fit the image of the cunning Russian oligarch he fancied himself.

After Ben's cover was blown, Ivan could have had him popped on any number of occasions, but he hadn't. No, he'd wanted to make a game out of it. A hunting game, with Ben as the prey and a quarter-million dollars as the prize. In essence, he'd made sure there wasn't any place in Atlanta Ben might be safe.

The agency had put him on permanent desk duty

and wanted him to transfer to another regional office, but Ben resisted, so they cut him loose altogether. His use as an undercover agent was spent. When Masters County found itself without a sheriff due to fallout from a sting operation targeting methamphetamine production, a friend of a friend gave Henry Masters his name. "The rest was history," he said, reaching for the remote control on the cushion beside him.

The screen went blank with the touch of a button, but Ben didn't move from the couch. He was half-afraid to go to bed. What if he spent the night replaying bloody scenes from dead-end streets of Zone 3? What if he lay awake thinking about Marlee Masters's long, bare legs? He snorted at the last thought.

Of course he was going to think about Marlee Masters's legs.

What had Lori said about Jeff Masters's death being too similar to Clint Young's? The two men had been friends once. Or so Lori had indicated. Had they veered off in different directions? Young started working for Timber Masters prior to Jeff Masters's death. Perhaps the two of them would have become friends again. Would Marlee Masters have come back to town if her brother had lived?

With a groan, he shook his head to clear the spiderweb of thoughts, set the bottle on the table, switched the television on again and stretched out on his side on the sofa. Better to spend the evening zoning out on cold cases and waking up with a crick in his neck than to lay awake chasing ghosts and elusive women.

"MORNING, BOSS MAN," Lori called out when he shuffled through the door the following morning. "You're up early."

Ben was dressed and mobile, but he wasn't necessarily awake. He cast a baleful glance at the empty coffeepot. How anyone made it through an overnight without coffee was beyond his powers of comprehension, but he didn't have the energy to question the woman's life choices.

"I'll give you Schaeffer's stapler if you'll make a coffee-and-doughnut run," he said as he trudged past her desk.

Lori narrowed her dark eyes appraisingly. "The good one? The Swingline?" she pressed.

He nodded as he dropped heavily into his seat. "Yep, but I'm holding it in escrow until I get some decent caffeine in me."

She moved to the coffee maker Julianne had banned him from operating in his first week on the job and gave it a fond pat. "I'll do you a double solid if you'll wait until I come in this afternoon to tell Schaeffer about the redistribution," she countered.

"Done."

With practiced ease, Lori set a pot to brewing. "I want to make it clear I'm doing this because I want the stapler, and I want to see Mike's face when you tell him it's mine. Gender has nothing to do with it."

Ben nodded his understanding. "And I want to make it clear I wasn't asking because you're a woman, but because you are on the approved list of coffee makers."

"Noted," she said as she hit the switch and the machine burbled to life. "Okay, I'll run and grab an immediate infusion for you. Do you want one dozen cliché-makers or two?"

"One," he said gruffly. "And if you order at least one cream-filled, I'll ask Julianne to order some of those colored paper clips."

"Done." She raised a hand as she beat a path to the door. "Okay, but I expect them to be jumbo-sized."

Ben nodded. "Noted." Watching her go, he made one last attempt to gain the upper hand in their dealings. "Make it two cream-filled doughnuts," he shouted after her.

Lori laughed, and he closed his gritty eyes, rubbing them with his thumb and forefinger. He heard the creak of hinges but figured it was the door closing in Lori's wake.

"Wow. Hitting the cream-filleds hard. I take it you didn't sleep much either?"

The plush softness of Marlee Masters's voice set him off like a starter's pistol. He kicked out, sending his desk chair flying across the tile floor. He crashed into the wall, arms flailing as momentum pitched him forward in his seat. He grunted and bit back an oath when the back of his hand connected with a metal filing cabinet. He shot out of his death trap of a chair, cradling his throbbing hand in the palm of the uninjured one. "Ms. Masters," he managed to huff.

"Oh, Sheriff, I'm sorry," she said, moving farther into the room. She drew to a stop just shy of touching him, then looked up into his face. "I didn't mean to startle you. I thought you heard me say hello to Lori," she said in a rush.

"I, uh, no," he managed to mutter. He shook his head, hoping the action would pull double duty by negating her assumption and clearing the fog from his brain. "No. Sorry, I didn't."

"You had doughnuts on your mind."

She wore running shorts. The strappy top she paired with them may as well have been a second skin. To add insult to injury, the mile-long legs he'd spent half the night purposefully not imagining were on display. She had cordless earbuds in her ears, but she wasn't shouting, so he assumed the phone strapped to her bicep wasn't cranking out the beats. He pressed his fingers to his throbbing temple in a vain attempt to block the mental image of her jogging down his street in her T-shirt and panties.

"Were you out running?"

She glanced down at the toes of her running shoes, then pushed a hand to her rib cage as she caught her breath. "Wow, you really do have what it takes to make detective, Kinsella," she quipped. "What gave me away?"

Ignoring her flippancy, he shook his head again, this time in disbelief. "Seriously? You've got some creeper peeping in your windows at night, then you're going out running all over town alone?"

"I'm assuming you mean like a person who jogs for exercise," she said, enunciating each word.

Ben copped to her meaning and cringed as he played the question back in his mind. If he'd had even a couple hours of escape into sleep, he might not have blundered into caveman territory, but damn, her legs were enough to make a man lose his ever-lovin' mind.

"I, uh…" Mortifyingly aware there was no way he could retract or redirect his misstep, he tried a different tack. "It's barely light outside. You shouldn't run with—" He gestured to her ears. Then, his instincts for self-preservation finally sprang to life. Holding up both hands in surrender, he squashed the chorus line of admonishments kicking its way through his mind. "Yeah, I didn't sleep much. Sorry for being old-fashioned." Then, quickly shifting topics, he asked, "What can I do for you?"

The corner of her mouth tilted upward. "Much better."

She huffed a breath, apparently as annoyed as he by the tension between them. Ben admired the effort, but watching her chest rise and fall did absolutely nothing to get his mind right.

"I came to talk to you about my brother," she said, jolting him from his wayward thoughts.

"Your brother?"

"Yes." She shifted her startlingly direct blue gaze to the file cabinet he'd assaulted. "I'm sure you've heard about my brother's death."

It was a statement, not a question. A leading one, but a statement nonetheless. Uncertain how to proceed, he opted for the less-is-more approach. "Yes."

A small harrumph of disgust escaped her. The resigned set of her jaw told him she'd expected nothing less but had still hoped for more.

"Small town," he said gruffly.

"Microscopic," she concurred.

"And I am the sheriff."

"Then, if you are acquainted with the circumstances surrounding my brother's...passing," she said with a hitch in her voice, "I'm sure you've heard that Jeff and Clint Young were friends when they were boys."

Lowering his arms, he nodded. "Yes."

"They hadn't been close in years," she hurried on. "People are making all sorts of assumptions—"

"Assumptions?" he prompted, interrupting her mid-stream.

"About connections between their deaths," she said, meeting his eyes directly again.

"Deputy Cabrera told me she was involved with your brother. While it's possible for someone to be interested in more than one person, I didn't get the impression there was any question in her mind she was the only one."

"You trust her judgment," Marlee determined.

Though she wasn't asking, he nodded anyway. "I haven't known her long, but in the short time I've been here, I have found Deputy Cabrera to be a quick study and a good judge of character. I trust her gut." He added the last because, to his way of thinking, what she'd said was all that needed to be said on the matter.

He gestured for her to take the seat opposite his desk and waited until she'd settled into the chair, then reclaimed his own. Rolling back to his desk, he bit the inside of his cheek to keep from wincing when he reached into his shirt pocket with his sore hand.

He pulled out the notebook he kept there and flipped it open to a blank page. "Was there something you wanted to tell me about your brother's death?"

She wet her lips, then glanced away, her gaze traveling over the postings and notices pinned to a corkboard. "My mother always said he didn't do it."

She spoke so softly, he scooted to the edge of his chair, hoping proximity would improve his chances of catching every word. "Your mother?"

"No doubt you've heard some whispers about her as well."

He had, but he'd be damned if he'd confirm or deny what he may or may not have heard about Henry Masters's beautiful but fragile wife. When he didn't answer, she continued her perusal of the room, refusing to look straight at him.

"My mother drinks too much," she said at last. "She's…" Again, she wet her lips, but this time she met his gaze head-on. "She's not in the most stable place right now."

"I understand," he assured her. No mother should have to bury a child. He couldn't imagine the pain of it. It was unfathomable.

"She has always said Jeff did not take his own life." This time, her voice was dull, and when he studied her, he saw signs of her sleepless night shadowing her lovely face.

"Has she any—"

"Proof?" she interrupted. Marlee shook her head forcefully. "No. Not one shred. Don't you think if there were any indication of anything untoward in the death of Henry Masters's son, a more extensive investigation would have taken place?"

The edge in her voice surprised him, but Ben was careful not to let it show. "No. I have no doubt."

"He would have spent every last penny he had on an investigation if there had been even a hint of something concrete, but there wasn't. My brother put a gun to his head and pulled the trigger."

Her voice was flat and emotionless, but when he searched her eyes, he saw only the anguish of the helpless there. "I *am* sorry for your loss," he said gently.

She tried to smirk and couldn't quite pull it off. "You didn't know him, Sheriff," she began.

"Ben," he interjected.

Marlee inclined her head, accepting his invitation to use his given name. "He was an ass," she said, a wicked light sparkling in her eyes. "Your typical spoiled, entitled prince of a small town."

Her blunt assessment made him warm to her even more. "But he was your brother and you loved him."

"From the moment they brought him home from the hospital," she said without hesitation.

"So you came here this morning to tell me…what?"

Marlee uncrossed her legs and bit her lip as she slid up to sit on the edge of the seat, rubbing her flat palms together between her knees. "I came here to tell you my mother might be a fragile flower hell-bent on drowning her grief, but I'm not."

"I can see you aren't."

"Yet my mama and I agree on one thing—I don't think my brother killed himself."

"What makes you say so?"

"I feel it in my gut," she said evenly.

He blinked, then shook his head. "Didn't I hear you're an attorney? I'd think the whole thing about evidence would have been covered in even the most basic law class."

She nodded and then stood. "It was. And I don't have any evidence. At least not yet."

The door opened, and they both clammed up as Lori backed her way into the office, a tray of coffee cups perched atop the doughnut box. "The place was packed," she called out without looking up. "Everyone's talking—"

"I don't doubt it," Marlee said with a short laugh.

Lori drew up short, then set her load down on the nearest desk. "Oh. I didn't realize you were coming in here."

"I stopped by to pass a couple messages from the family to Sheriff Kinsella," Marlee answered smoothly. "Today is my first day as chief legal counsel at Timber Masters. I thought I'd get a jump on things." She tugged the hem of her tank down over her hips. "I'd better get my run in before I'm late punching in."

Ben had to use all his strength of will to keep his eyes glued to her face. Her expression was one of calm friendliness, but the intensity in her eyes told him she didn't want to air her suspicions in front of Lori.

"Yes, thank you." He cleared his throat, desperate to buy some time to figure out what she expected him to do with the groundless suppositions she'd dumped on him. "You'll call if there's anything more I can do?"

"Absolutely."

"Doughnut?" Lori offered, opening the box in invitation.

Marlee peered into the box, then tossed a triumphant glance over her shoulder. "Are those cream-filled?"

He scowled to indicate he wasn't buying the wide-eyed innocent bit. "Weren't you going for a run?"

She narrowed her gaze, and he realized a fraction of a second too late that she believed his reminder to be a challenge.

"Oh, Sheriff, if there's one thing I learned in law school, it was how to eat on the run."

With a smirk, she plucked one of his precious cream-filled pastries from the box and bit into it as she waved her thanks to Lori and hustled out the door.

Chapter Six

Marlee smiled as her father's longtime secretary, Mrs. Devane, came out from behind her desk to greet her with a handclasp. "So good to see you, dear. We're excited to have you on board."

She wasn't on board, but there was no way Marlee could say so to poor sweet Mrs. Devane. The woman had been guarding the executive offices of Timber Masters since Marlee's grandfather ran the place. She settled on something innocuous but polite. "Good morning, Mrs. Devane. I'm happy to see you too."

"Your father is waiting for you," the older woman cooed.

Marlee felt her press something hard into the center of her palm and looked down to find a cellophane-wrapped butterscotch candy in her hand. The kind she used to sneak to them on the rare occasions when Marlee and Jeff came into the offices with their father. Hot tears stung her eyes, and her throat closed. Looking at the polished oak door her great-grandfather had made with his own hands, she felt a wave of longing for her brother threatening to swallow her.

Mrs. Devane patted the hand holding the candy. "You'll be the next Masters at the helm of Timber Masters," she said with quiet conviction. "I suppose it would be more appropriate for you to call me Gladys now."

Marlee gulped the lump in her throat. "Thank you, Mrs. Devane."

The other woman chortled as she headed back to her post. "We'll work on it. Young Jeffrey almost had it down when he—" Gladys's eyes widened as her brain caught up to her mouth, and Marlee noticed the sheen of moisture trapped behind the other woman's spectacles. "You go on in, dear," she said, her voice thick and hushed. "They're waiting for you."

Anxious to escape, Marlee failed to register the plural pronoun prior to opening the door and stepping into the confines of her father's inner sanctum. She drew up short when she saw Henry seated in one of the club chairs facing his desk rather than the massive leather seat behind it. He was sharing a low chuckle with the white-haired man seated in the matching chair. Both men looked up, and Marlee recognized the town's resident attorney, Wendell Wingate, by the polka-dot bow tie he wore with his pale gray summer-weight suit.

"Miss Marlee," the older man called out, admiration lacing the greeting.

He braced both hands on the arms of his chair to rise, but she tried to wave him off. "Oh, no, Mr. Wingate. No need to get up. I'm sorry to interrupt. Mrs. Devane said to come in. It's nice to see you again."

Mr. Wingate pushed to his feet and captured her

hands between his. "The day I don't get up when a pretty woman enters a room is the day your daddy can build me a nice pine box." He beamed at her. "Congratulations on your graduation, my dear, and welcome to the club," he added with a wink.

"Thank you, sir." She extracted her hands from his grasp then gestured for him to sit again. "Would you prefer I came back in a while?"

Henry shook his head. "No. I called Wendell in for you."

He rose from his chair, then gestured for Marlee to take it. Tamping down on her disappointment, Marlee seated herself. "Oh?"

"Yes, it only makes sense." Her father settled himself in the executive chair behind the massive desk. "Wendell has been handling the company's legal matters for decades, but now we have you."

A surge of panic had Marlee fighting the urge to jump from her seat. To counteract it, she folded her hands in her lap and waited patiently, exactly as her mother had taught her. "You can't mean that," she said with a nervous chuckle.

"Unceremoniously fired," the older man said with a woeful shake of his head.

Appalled, Marlee gaped at her father. "But after so many years—"

He cut off her protest with a nonchalant wave of his hand. "Stop preying on the girl's sympathies, Wendell," he admonished. Focusing on her, he said only, "This has been the plan all along. Wendell here has his eye on a seat on the bench."

"Oh." She blinked twice as she felt another chance at charting her own course closing down on her.

If the only attorney in town wasn't on retainer to Timber Masters, they'd have to engage someone from another county for counsel. Henry Masters didn't give company business to anyone living outside the county that bore his family's name. She cast about for something to say as her mind fought to recalibrate plans.

"You're closing your practice?"

Mr. Wingate shook his head. "No. My grandson, Simon, has been with a lobbying firm in Atlanta, but he'll be coming home to take over the firm."

Marlee stared at him in shock. Wonder of wonders, Simon Wingate was coming to Pine Bluff. Wendell Wingate's son, Dell Wingate, had been serving the district that encompassed Masters County in the Georgia General Assembly since the year after his twenty-first birthday. Dell's son, Simon, used to visit Pine Bluff for two full weeks every summer, but as far as Marlee was aware, he hadn't stepped foot in the town since the day his teenage rebellion won out over the wishes of his grandparents. Not even for his grandmother's funeral. The snub had fueled the gossips for years after the event. He'd been in college then, Marlee recalled. At Yale. Another strike against him as far as the people around here were concerned.

"Wow. Simon. I don't think I've seen him since I was in middle school."

Wendell nodded, his genial smile fixed firmly in place, though it didn't reach his eyes. "Yes, I think you would be about right." He hesitated a moment, seeming to have lost his usual bluff and bluster. "But, boy, wait until he gets a look at you, young lady." He winked at Henry. "Perhaps we can orchestrate a merger."

Henry huffed a laugh but rolled his eyes. "Keep your sights set on the circuit court. You do more good for us in the superior court than as a matchmaker."

Wingate chuckled and cast a long-suffering sigh in Marlee's direction. "See how it is? His daddy would tan his hide if he ever heard him disrespecting his elders thataway."

Marlee couldn't help being amused at the byplay between the two men and the image of her quiet, kind grandfather ever getting the best of his bossy son. Still, she could play the game too. "Mama always says he's incorrigible."

"An understatement," the older man concurred.

"Enough," Henry grumbled. "Marlee, you're going to spend some time over at Wendell's offices. I need you to get up to speed as quickly as possible, and I can't pull him away from all the drunk and disorderlies he's set to defend."

"Hey, now, the majority of my clients are employees of this fine company," Wendell shot back.

Her father's gaze drifted down to the stack of folders arranged on the corner of his desk, and Marlee gathered he was losing interest in the conversation now that he'd given his order. "Exactly why I need to get back to running this business."

"I don't want to be in the way," Marlee said, dividing a glance between the two men as she searched for an escape hatch.

"You won't be," they said in unison.

Taken aback by how quickly and efficiently her father had managed to circumvent her every plan, Marlee dug in. "I understand you have a plan," she said tightly. "But I was hoping to discuss something with you in private this morning."

Her eyes bore into the top of her father's head, but he didn't notice.

Mr. Wingate, obviously accustomed to taking his cues from this man two decades his junior, rose from his chair. "I'll give the two of you a moment," he said as he buttoned his suit jacket.

"Not necessary," her father answered, shuffling through the stack of folders, his mind fixed on his next task.

She bit the inside of her cheek to keep from screaming for his attention, as she had when she was a child. But she wasn't a child any longer. And she wasn't one of Henry Masters's many pawns. Tipping her chin up, she drizzled extra honey over her words. "If you wouldn't mind, Mr. Wingate. Please and thank you."

The second the older man opened the office door, her father looked up from his work, impatience etched into every line on his face. "There's no need to keep the man waiting, Marlee. His time is valuable, and you'd better believe he's billing us for every minute of it."

"I understand, but I need to tell you—"

"You think you want to get a job up in Atlanta," he said, cutting her off. He lifted his head and met her eyes with a pointed stare. "But you don't."

"I do," she argued.

"There's nothing for you there," he said succinctly.

The steely glint in his steady blue gaze made her gut twist. Pressure built in her chest. Her fight-or-flight instincts kicked into gear, and Marlee exhaled as she realized her father had somehow gotten to Jared Baker. Her fingertips tingled, but her hands felt tight and numb as she curled them into fists. If he'd managed to poison Baker against hiring her, Henry wouldn't have thought twice about doing the same with every other decent firm in town. Now he had the nerve to sit there glaring at her as if she'd run over his dog then got out of her car and kicked the carcass.

"There's nothing for me here."

"Your place is here," he replied, his voice quiet and uninflected. "That was the deal, wasn't it? I send you to law school, and then you come back here to work for me."

No, the deal had been she'd go to law school then come back to help her brother run the company. But their plan could never happen now. Neither would her new dream of a life free of Timber Masters and all that being one of the Masterses of Masters County entailed. Not as long as her father lived, at least.

Snapping her jaw shut, she rose and stalked to the door. When she reached for the knob, he called after her, "Don't you want to guess what I told them?"

She didn't want to give him the satisfaction, but she needed to determine if the situation might be salvageable. "What?"

"I told them I wanted them to liaise with you on

Timber Masters's franchising along the Eastern Seaboard."

Whirling to face him, she gaped at the audacity of the play. "Franchising? We're not the kind of business that can be easily franchised."

"We are aware of that, but Jared Baker doesn't have the first clue about my business. Either way, he was happy to swap a first-year associate for a chance to even talk about it. And I'm such a friendly guy and all," he said, gesturing expansively. "We're having drinks the next time I'm in Atlanta." He picked up his pen and tapped the file in front of him, tsking softly. "So there you have it. You're worth about two fingers of Glenlivet on the open market."

"Wait a minute—"

"No," he barked. "I won't wait another second. I paid for your degree so you'd put it to work for me. And don't you keep Wendell waiting another moment, missy. You hear?"

SHE SEETHED THE entire morning, miles from absorbing any of the words flowing from Wingate's mouth. They hardly mattered anyway. She could read. Once she had the files at her disposal, she'd figure the business out on her own. At the moment, she wasn't the least bit interested in learning anything her father's toady had to teach her.

"Miss Marlee?" he called, gently breaking into her ruminations.

When she looked up, he closed the file he'd been

droning on about, then fixed her with a kindly gaze. "Many people would kill to be in your position."

"Excuse me?"

Though she had been woolgathering, Marlee had heard the man perfectly. She simply wasn't sure how to respond when people said stuff like that to her. People assumed she led a charmed life, but they didn't have any idea how it felt to be Marlee Masters.

"The first thing they taught us in school was to assume nothing, Mr. Wingate."

"We're colleagues now, Marlee," he said, peering at her over the top of his tortoiseshell reading glasses. "Call me Wendell."

She hesitated, transfixed by the warmth and… Did she see understanding in his brown eyes? "I'm not sure I can," she confessed with an apologetic wince.

"Try it on for size. I'm sure it'll grow on you."

He said the last with such supreme confidence, she had to laugh. "I imagine it will… Wendell."

"It's my grandson's name too," he said conversationally.

To her recollection, the Wingates had only one son and one grandson. Puzzled, she gave her head a shake. "Simon's?"

He nodded. "Wendell Simon Wingate the Third," he intoned sonorously.

"'The Third'?" she repeated. "All three of you are Wendell Simon Wingate?"

"Dell nabbed the nickname, and Simon's mother categorically objected to calling her only child 'Trey' or 'Chip' or any of the other inanities used to differentiate generations, so Simon it was."

"I see."

"And I see too." He removed the reading glasses and folded the temples in, then used them to point at her. "I see you clearly. I also saw your brother. I see your mother, your father, and I knew your grandfather about as well as any two men could know one another outside of getting biblical." He halted a moment, his dark eyes steady on hers. "And I too can differentiate between the generations without the use of silly nicknames."

He couldn't have driven his point home harder if he'd used a judge's gavel. Still, the man was quite obviously and unapologetically in her father's pocket. Determined to proceed with caution, she gave him nothing more than a mildly interested, "Oh?"

"You and your brother were wary of your father's plans and machinations. Hell, I often chafe against them myself, but I can tell you one thing—the man knows how to run a business."

"I've never doubted my father's business acumen," she said flatly.

"Only his affection."

His blunt assessment threw her off balance. "What's your point?"

Wendell set his glasses atop the file he'd been trying to go over with her and folded his hands in front of him. "My point is, you can disagree with him, you can rebel and run away, you can denounce the name of Masters at the top of your lungs… Your father is a horse's patoot most of the time, Marlee, but one day you will inherit all of this whether you want it or not."

She blinked, taken aback. "He could leave it to someone else," she argued. "Doesn't he have some second-in-command he can bless with it?"

"He won't."

"He could sell it, stick Mama in rehab and take off for Las Vegas."

"He won't run away either."

"I don't want it." She pushed back from the gleaming conference table, where they'd been seated adjacent to one another.

"He won't care whether you do or not," he reminded her. "You are a Masters. The last of the line," he added with a sad twist of his lips. "I had a similar talk with your brother when he was finishing up school. You were born to be who you are, Marlee. You can't change who or what shaped you in the past. You can only pin your hopes on the people who come after. Your father has been doing so since the day you were born."

"Since the day Jeff was born, you mean," she said with a bitter bark of a laugh. "He forgot all about me once he had his heir apparent."

Wendell sat back in his chair, cocking his head to the side. "Funny how you never blamed Jeff," he observed.

"It wasn't Jeff's fault."

"True, but rational thought rarely plays a starring role when it comes to family dynamics." His expression grew sorrowful and his eyes misty. "Jeff and I talked about this."

"You did?" She wasn't certain what he was referring to, but she leaned in, hungry for any scrap of the brother she missed so much.

The older man nodded, his gaze fixed somewhere in the distance. "He told me his kids would never wonder if he loved the company more than he loved them. Told me he'd sell it off right down to the last toothpick to reassure them."

"His kids," she whispered, devastated by the tragic loss of her imaginary nieces and nephews. "He wanted kids."

Wendell sat up straighter, shaking his head to clear it. "Yes, well. The what-ifs are what makes it all so sad, aren't they? The might-have-beens."

"Should-have-beens," she corrected.

He nodded. "Yes. It's often the loss of possibilities that breaks our hearts." Picking up his glasses, he deftly unfolded them and shoved them up onto the end of his nose. "But we deal in facts, don't we?" he said, shifting forward in his chair again.

Marlee couldn't resist probing one more time. "Do you think Jeff killed himself, Mr. Wingate?"

The older man reared back, but he couldn't quite pull off the appearance of genuine surprise she assumed he was hoping for.

Narrowing her eyes, she pressed harder. "You don't, do you?"

"What I think does not matter," he chided. "We are only concerned with what the evidence at hand will support. All we know for certain is two promising young men are dead, presumably by their own hand."

"But you think it's odd, don't you?" she insisted.

"Jeff and Clint Young were friends once, they both worked for Timber Masters—"

He cut her off. "Their place of employment is hardly a strong connection in this instance. Most of the residents of Masters County are employed by Timber Masters or adjacent companies." She opened her mouth to say more, but he held up his hand to halt the flow. "And we were all friends with our peers when we were young, but we tend to grow apart as our lives progress. I seem to remember you and Mandy Duncan were thick as thieves when you were in high school. What's she up to these days?"

Marlee blinked, thrown by having the tables reversed on her so deftly. "She's still living here in town, isn't she?"

He inclined his head in a half nod. "She is. As a matter of fact, she works for Timber Masters," he added with a triumphant lift of his unruly eyebrows.

Pursing her lips, Marlee inhaled deeply through her nose as she prepared to concede. "Fine. Point taken."

Wendell flipped a couple of pages without looking at them. "But I did hear she had a date lined up with Clint Young for the weekend after he died," he said, glancing up at last. "I find it interesting he'd made plans to take Mandy out but decided to end it all instead."

The implication hung between them for a moment. He pursed his lips, then said, "Perhaps I took the wrong approach with this. Rather than diving straight into Timber Masters itself, maybe we should start somewhat smaller and build up so you can get a feel for the scope of the work."

He thumbed through a stack of folders to his right, then withdrew one bulging with papers. "These are summary files, you understand," he explained as he plopped the brick of a file on the table in front of her. "There are boxes and boxes of documents to back all this up, but I keep the most pertinent facts close at hand."

"Real estate?" She eyed him askance as she flipped open the cover. "You want to start me off with lease agreements and evictions?"

"Among other things," he said, unperturbed by her pique. "I'm sure you are aware your family has extensive holdings throughout the county. Commercial, single family and multidwelling rental properties are held in a separate corporation from the business or personal properties."

Despite her annoyance at being handed the legal equivalent of a bike with training wheels, she scanned the summary pages, her lips parting as she lined up her questions. Skimming to the bottom of the page, she clamped her mouth shut and forced her pride aside long enough to absorb the information. "Nearly all of our tenants in single-family dwellings were evicted two years ago."

"Yes, they were." Wendell beamed at her, and for some reason it made Marlee feel like she'd earned her first gold star.

"Why? They couldn't have all lost their checkbooks at once."

He chuckled and shook his head. "No. I wish it

were a simple matter of failure to pay." He pointed to the file. "Take a look at the yellow papers. Those are original copies of work orders."

She did as she was told. But as she studied the notes about tests administered and failed, remediation of "residential chemical contamination" and certifications secured once the work was done, she wagged her head in confusion.

"Did we build on a toxic waste dump or something?" Marlee had heard her father complain about the Environmental Protection Agency and the costs incurred by following their guidelines her entire life, but building on contaminated land would be a bridge too far, even for Henry.

"No." The older man took a deep breath, then released it with a shuddering sigh. "The Drug Enforcement Agency cut a big swath through this part of the state a couple years ago," he began.

Marlee recalled her father and Jeff talking about the agency's action in Masters and surrounding counties. "Yes. They were looking for people producing methamphetamine, weren't they?"

The older man nodded. "Precisely."

When he said nothing more, she glanced down at the paper in the folder. The puzzle pieces slipped into place. "They were cooking in our houses."

"A number of them, yes." Wendell ruffled a stack of papers with the side of his thumb before proceeding with caution. "When your brother first came to work, your father had put Jeff in charge of overseeing the real estate division."

He let the tidbit of information dangle. Frowning, Marlee slipped her foot out of her pump and swung the shoe on her toes, a nervous habit she'd picked up while being forced to sit through dozens of white tablecloth–draped debutante teas. She flexed her foot faster and faster as she flipped through page after page of documentation. Many of them carried her brother's signature scrawled at the bottom.

"Jeff?" She froze for a moment. "He wasn't involved with drugs, was he?"

Wendell shook his head. "No. The only thing your brother was guilty of was being young and naive." He straightened in his seat. "He acted in good faith, but a number of people around him did not. There were some who escaped prosecution on technicalities. Some, your brother might have considered friends at one time. Adding insult to injury, it galled Jeff to see the real estate division bankrupted on his watch. A fact your father didn't hesitate to remind him of at every opportunity."

Marlee's gut churned and her foot started to twitch again, the leather edges of her pump knocking against the bottom of her heel.

Wendell pushed on, but now he sat still, his gaze fixed on her. "To make amends, he negotiated a deal where they could sell off a chunk of the family's personal property. A parcel earmarked to come to him eventually anyway."

Dread pooled in the depths of her belly. "What property?"

"An attorney representing land development trust made a large offer for several parcels of land out on Sawtooth Lake."

Chapter Seven

Marlee sat at the conference table piled with files.
Wendell had abandoned her for a client meeting, so
she sat there leafing through countless pages of title
transfers, lease agreements and other assorted documentation related to both the sale of the lake property
and the remediation of the rental properties in town,
wondering what the hell had happened to her hometown in the years since she'd left for college.

In her mind, Pine Bluff was the quintessential small
Southern town. They had pancake breakfasts after
church on Sundays and parades for almost every holi-
day. There were ice-cream socials and sewing circles
with multiple generations of women from the same
family as members. Sure, people moved away, but for
some reason or another, a good portion of those people
eventually found their way back.

What they didn't have were people who manufac-
tured illicit drugs in their kitchens and massive distri-
bution networks stretching across the state and beyond.

Or so she had thought.

Her mind reeling, she continued flipping pages, trying to focus on the real estate holdings she was supposed to be studying. But here and there she found references to the tenants who were caught up in the legal proceedings stemming from the DEA sting. So many people involved in something she—a Masters from Masters County—had no idea was even happening. It didn't seem possible.

Her father had raised his children to believe their family name made them personally responsible for the health and well-being of every person who lived inside the county lines, but reading through these files, she began to realize her hometown and its surrounding area were not the bucolic microcosms she'd believed them to be.

Some of the statements taken as part of the evictions read like works of fiction. Who would have ever believed Clem Watkins, the man who'd been janitor at the high school as long as anyone could remember, was one of the biggest dealers in town? And he'd been savvy enough to cut a deal with the agency in exchange for a handful of underlings and the name of the man who'd gotten him started in the business.

Clint Young.

But both the agents working the lingering cases and the prosecutor's office had been unable to unearth a shred of evidence to support Clem's claim, and no charges had ever been filed against Clint.

As far as Marlee could see, he'd managed to cover any involvement he might have had so thoroughly, he hadn't even been brought in for formal questioning. Did Ben Kinsella suspect Clint was involved in all this mess, even peripherally? Was he aware Masters County was such an unholy mess when he'd agreed to take the job as sheriff? Were the surrounding counties as much of a mess? Prescott County bordered Sawtooth Lake as well. Who had cleaned up over there? Prescott County's economy was driven by small-crop farmers, some who grew timber to sell to Timber Masters or direct to the paper mills. They didn't have the backing of one solid, stable company. Masters County had Timber Masters and the Masters family. Who was footing the bill for Prescott's recovery?

Closing one file folder, she reached for another labeled Sawtooth Lake Sportsmen's Club and opened it with some trepidation. Wendell had told her Henry had rejected Jeff's idea of selling off parcels of their property out of hand, but in the weeks following her brother's death, he'd reconsidered. Back in the day, there had only been two dwellings on the lake—her family's and the one built by Clint Young's father.

Four bedrooms with adjoining baths, a chef's kitchen and a wraparound deck affording spectacular sunset views made her family's spread a showplace. The extensive use of good Georgia pine and rough-hewn wood accents allowed her father to call it a cabin rather than a lake house—a distinction Henry had found appealing, even if the rest of the family couldn't have cared less.

He primarily used the place for entertaining clients, or loaned it out to people he thought might be influential or beneficial to the business. Her mother had hated it out there and had grudgingly gone only when Henry put his foot down. She and Jeff swam in the lake when they were young, though she preferred a nice chlorinated pool to anything with a mud bottom and slimy grass that wrapped around a person's legs. If she closed her eyes and focused hard, she could conjure up a happy memory or two, but they were sparse.

She couldn't figure out why it upset her so to discover the land adjacent to theirs had been sold. Opening the folder, she inspected the revised plats dividing the property into five sections. The largest belonged to their family. Their closest neighbors were still the Youngs.

Theirs had actually been a cabin. A simple place built by Mr. Young as an escape from his unhappy home life. There were three other parcels situated on the other side of a cove from the Masters and Young places. They were labeled with names. Pulling the yellow legal pad closer, she noted them.

Thomason, Abernathy and Baker.

She tapped her pen against the pad until something clicked. Abernathy. She'd dated a boy named Bo Abernathy in high school. It was possible his parents had purchased one of the plots, but it didn't seem likely. The family wasn't particularly well-off. Dismissing the name as coincidence, she checked the next. There were three different Baker families in the area, to her recollection. She marked it for further research, then sat staring into space as she ran through her mental map of town. For the life of her, she couldn't place anyone named Thomason but had the niggling suspicion she ought to recognize the name.

Wendell opened the door to the small room where

she'd spread out and popped his head in. "Doing all right in here?"

"Is there a Thomason family in town?" She bit her lip as she searched her memory again, trying to place anyone she may have met with the name.

"Family? No." Wendell paused, his expression thoughtful. "You mean other than Will Thomason, right?"

"Who is Will Thomason?"

"Will Thomason," Wendell repeated. "General manager at Timber Masters," he added with a pointed stare.

"I don't know a Will Thomason," Marlee said. "I thought Jeff was the general manager."

"Yes, he was, but…" He let the thought trail off and made a vague circling motion with his hand.

"But Jeff is dead," she concluded flatly. "Will Thomason is the man who took his place."

Wendell rolled his shoulders back, then cocked his head as he studied her. "Come to think of it, I suppose Will moved while you were in college." He frowned. "I'd have thought your father would have introduced you, but then, you haven't been home long."

"No. I haven't." She closed the file with a sigh. "I guess a lot of things have changed since I've been gone."

"Some things but not everything," Wendell said gently. "You're past due for some lunch. Go walk around town and clear your head a bit. I believe you'll find the onion rings at the Daisy Drive-In are as tasty as they ever were."

She hooked her arm through her handbag and rose,

anxious to leave the files behind. "Can I bring you anything?"

"No, thank you. Miss Delia has packed me my no-salt, no-fat, no-flavor lunch, and she reports back to my daughter-in-law if I try to cheat."

She grinned as she imagined the Wingate's five-foot-nothing housekeeper giving the old man what for. "How would she know?"

He chuckled. "Another thing that hasn't changed. Word travels fast around here. She'd sense it if I even dipped a french fry into the ketchup."

Marlee stilled, her hand on the door handle. He was right. The only mill in Masters County that ran faster than her daddy's lumber mill was the rumor mill. It was time to pound the pavement, and possibly press an ear to the ground.

BEN WAS BITING into one of the Daisy Drive-In's famous mile-high club sandwiches when the door to the office swung open and Marlee Masters blew in. He lowered the sandwich to the carryout container and forced himself to chew as she approached. When she drew to a stop in front of his desk, he swallowed with a hard gulp then reached for the cup of sweet tea he'd ordered to go with his lunch, gesturing for his guest to take a seat while he washed the food down.

Holding a to-go cup of her own, Marlee dropped into the wooden guest chair so hard he winced. "Ms. Masters. We meet again," he said, wiping his mouth with one of the inconsequential paper napkins the dairy bar had provided with the meal. "What can I do for you this time?"

Marlee glanced over both shoulders as if she'd only now noticed they weren't alone in the office. Julianne was at home eating her own lunch, but Deputy Mike Schaeffer sat at his desk, his pen frozen in midair. The younger man gaped at Marlee in wide-eyed shock, and it was all Ben could do to suppress a smile. The woman did cause a stir.

"You can go grab your lunch early, Mike," Ben called out to him, his voice genial but the command clear.

He saw the younger man's desire to protest. After all, he'd come on shift only a half hour ago. But Ben had the distinct feeling he shouldn't have an audience around for whatever Ms. Masters wanted from him.

Ben waved his hand in a shooing motion. "It'll keep you from having to run out later." He cast a wistful glance at his uneaten lunch, then carefully closed the lid on the container.

"I'm sorry—I didn't mean to interrupt your lunch," she said. "I figured you'd be done. You must have had a busy morning too." She waved the cup in her hand, indicating she'd been to the Daisy as well. "I opted to drink my lunch. A chocolate malt has everything a girl needs to power through the afternoon." Her cheeks flushed a rosy pink, making her blue eyes appear even brighter. "Please, eat." She waved a hand at the container.

He was about to refuse when his stomach rumbled. Loudly. Marlee laughed, and he felt the heat rise in his own cheeks. "Excuse me," he mumbled. Pushing the sandwich aside, he sat up straighter. "You're going to think all I do is eat."

"Heaven forbid people consume meals at meal times," she countered.

He fixed her with a pointed look. "Is there something I can do for you?"

She scooted forward in her seat and placed her cup on the edge of his desk. "I wanted to ask you a couple of questions, if you don't mind."

Ben nodded, then popped the lip on the container again. "Wanna join the mile-high club with me?" He kept his expression sober but gestured to the quartered club sandwich nestled into a bed of potato chips.

Her lips parted as she looked at him, then down at the sandwich. "You get that from the Daisy?"

"Of course."

He could see she was sorely tempted, but still she refused. "No. Thank you. It looks delicious, though."

He pushed the box closer to her, then picked up the quarter he'd abandoned. "How is your first day going? Did you get a big office and everything?"

"I got farmed out," she said, her lips thinning into a line.

He froze, the stacked sandwich gripped in both hands and his mouth hanging open for a moment. Moving his head to the side, he peered at her around his lunch. "Farmed out?"

"To Wendell Wingate."

She gave a jerky shrug he supposed was meant to be nonchalance, but the tiny furrow between her eyes gave her away. It also annoyed him. Marlee Masters was a woman born to smile, not scowl.

"You've been working with Wendell? Well, I guess that makes sense in a way," he commented, manufacturing his own measure of casualness.

"Sheriff—"

"Ben," he corrected, then sank his teeth into the sandwich.

"I wanted to ask if you knew anything about the sweep the DEA made of this area a couple years ago," she continued.

Ben chewed methodically, examining the question in his mind and checking every angle before deciding how to answer. He swallowed, then took a sip of his tea. His response was nothing more than a cautious, "I do." He then took another healthy bite to buy more time.

She tipped her head to the side, clearly irritated by his succinct answer but prepared to reframe her question in a half dozen other ways.

"Fine. Can you tell me more about the actions surrounding the Drug Enforcement Agency's activities in this area and the fallout from them?"

He nodded again, his mouth full. He watched her practically vibrate with impatience as she waited, and he couldn't resist yanking her chain one more time. Though he acknowledged the necessary role attorneys played in their legal system, as a cop, he wasn't particularly crazy about them. If he was honest with himself, he would admit his willingness to help this one wasn't motivated by a simple desire to see justice served.

"I can." He chewed then swallowed before waving

his hand as if telling her to come at him. "Try again, but this time ask in a way that doesn't give me as much wiggle room."

She huffed her indignation, her face alight with a blush. "Fine. What do you know about the raids the DEA staged in this area?"

He tossed the crusts of the sandwich into the box and picked up another segment as he eyed her. "Two years ago, a team of agents undertook an operation to shut down one of the largest methamphetamine networks in the Southeast."

"You were part of the team?"

He ignored her shocked question in favor of getting the pertinent information out of the way. "Most of their operations centered in Masters and Prescott Counties. We made several arrests, turned several more of the operation's key figures into witnesses and shut down the majority of the production in the area."

"The majority but not all?" She nonchalantly picked up a corner of his sandwich and took a bite.

"These people are insidious. You can round up as many as you can, but there will always be others to take their place."

"So you're saying people around here are still producing and distributing methamphetamine?" she pressed, incredulous. "The population of those two counties combined is less than a decent-sized suburb. How many people can be involved?"

"There were over two hundred persons of interest named in the case."

"And you were involved? Working with the DEA?"

He shook his head. "Not directly. I worked for the agency but was assigned elsewhere."

"You were with the DEA?"

"Yes."

"As an agent?"

"Yes."

She gaped at him for a moment, then color rose in her cheeks. "Why are you here, then?" she demanded. "I mean, why did you leave?"

"Personal reasons," he said, though for some reason it cost him to maintain his usual calm demeanor when she was the person asking the questions.

Marlee's agitation filled the room. The air felt charged. Ionized. Like after a lightning strike. He sniffed, wondering if he'd catch a hint of ozone, but he didn't.

"Does my association with the DEA bother you?" He was taken aback by her reaction to discovering he'd once been a federal agent. Most people were impressed. Her father had been. But Marlee seemed... wary. He changed tactics. "Let me ask this—why does it bother you?"

"It doesn't," she answered a shade too quickly.

He set his section of sandwich aside, then leaned in, folding his arms on the desk. "It does. Why?"

She shot to her feet, and it was all Ben could do not to follow suit. After her morning visit, he'd done nothing but think about her and her brother. He'd even gone so far as to pull Jeffrey Masters's file and compare the notes taken by his predecessor with his own observations of the scene in the Youngs' cabin. They had only two things in common. First, the cause of death, noted as self-inflicted by Mel Schuler on both cases, and Jeff Masters's confirmed by the medical examiner's office in Macon. And second, the fact that both men took their lives in cabins on—

"I want you to come with me out to Sawtooth Lake this evening," Marlee broke into his thoughts.

He was still formulating a response when the office door opened and Mike strode in holding a take-out box of his own. His steps faltered inside the door, and Ben leaned over in his chair to peer around Marlee. "Can you give us a couple minutes more, Mike?"

"I, uh, sure," the younger man said. "I'll go, um… there's a bench in the square."

"Good idea," Ben agreed. "Enjoy some sunshine."

The thermometer had already zipped past the mid-eighties and was nudging ninety degrees, but Mike didn't protest. He simply left. Straightening, Ben maintained eye contact with Marlee, not speaking until the door closed again.

"Why do I get the feeling you're not asking me on a date?" he said at last.

She colored beautifully at the insinuation but pressed on. "There's something…off about all this. I feel it in my gut."

She pressed her palm flat against her stomach, and Ben lost the battle to maintain eye contact. Her long fingers splayed over her belly. Her fingernails were unpolished. It surprised him for some reason. Probably because most of the women he'd met with her means and social station kept themselves buffed and varnished to a high sheen. But not Marlee. He let his gaze travel over her, taking in the details of her slim skirt and silky blouse as he forced himself to look her in the face again. These clothes were elegant. Simple, but beautifully made and clearly expensive. Unlike the boxy blue suit she'd worn the first time he saw her, these pieces were tailored to nip in at all the key spots and allow for her generous curves in others. He got the distinct impression Marlee had not been the one to select this outfit.

He allowed his curiosity to get the better of him. "Who buys your clothes?"

The question caught her completely off guard. She actually took a small step back, wobbling on her high heels when she bumped into the chair she'd abandoned. "What?"

"Your clothes." He nodded toward her. "Whoever picked out this outfit wasn't the same person who bought the blue suit you wore the other day."

"I—" she started, then stopped. "I'm not a child," she snapped, fire flashing in her eyes and chagrin adding to the color in her cheeks. "I can dress myself."

"But the suit—"

"I'd just bought it. I didn't have time to have it altered," she explained in a rush. "Are you also the fashion police in these parts?"

"No, I'm a man who makes his living observing people and their actions." Tired of craning his neck to look up at her, he rose too. "The suit was some kind of a statement. I'm not sure who was supposed to get the message, but it spoke volumes."

She lifted her chin in defiance. "And what did it say?"

"It said you didn't want to be here. That you had other plans." Now staring down at her, he added, "Plans inconveniently interrupted by Clint Young's death."

"You think I'm so cold?" she said, slashing the air with her hand. "And Clint's death has nothing to do with anything."

"But you told me this morning it did," he reminded her. "You came trotting in here this morning telling me you think there's something connecting your brother's death with Young's."

She sucked in a sharp breath, then pressed those lush lips together.

He forced himself to soften his expression and relax his stance. They weren't on opposing sides of an issue, only on opposite sides of a desk. "Listen, I've been in law enforcement most of my adult life," he said, careful to avoid coming across as condescending. "I started out as military police, got recruited by the agency then came here. I've crossed paths and swords with a lot of lawyers in my time, but Miss Marlee, I think we both want the same thing here."

At least as far as her suspicions went, he amended only to himself. He was fairly certain Marlee Masters wasn't thinking about him the same way he thought about her.

When she didn't respond to his verbal olive branch, he sighed. "I'm only making observations because I'm trying to figure out the person I'm dealing with."

"By commenting on my clothes?"

"Isn't there some saying about clothes making the man? Or, in this case, woman?" He gestured to the chair she'd vacated, and she crossed her arms over her chest, her expression mulish. Figuring she was dug in, he changed his approach. "Why do you want me to go to the lake with you?"

"I don't think I do anymore."

Ben was sure she'd meant the words as a retort, but they came out with shades of sulkiness. Suddenly, he had absolutely no trouble reconciling the beautiful woman in front of him with the girl who undoubtedly ruled the school. Repressing a chuckle, he reclaimed his seat and reached for his lunch even though he'd lost his appetite.

When he didn't trip all over himself to convince her, she crumbled. "I thought since you saw the scene where Clint…died, you might get something out of seeing my family's cabin."

His brows knit as he wondered what could he gain from seeing the place where yet another young man had decided to end his life? And what could Marlee possibly stand to gain? Didn't she realize she'd have been a prime suspect if there'd been any hint of foul play in her brother's death? Then again, if a woman who had as much to lose as Marlee Masters was asking questions, shouldn't he be paying closer attention?

"Fine," he agreed, even though his brain hadn't quite finished processing her request. Still, he had no desire to take it back. "We can take my truck," he said, picking up another sad excuse for a paper napkin and crumpling it into his palm. "What time should I pick you up?"

Marlee shifted from one foot to the other, clearly surprised by his capitulation. Ben fought the urge to chuckle. He enjoyed keeping her off balance.

But she recovered quickly. "I'll meet you here. Will five thirty work? I want to run home and change." She waited a beat, then flashed him a saucy grin. "I can't wait to hear your breakdown on why I'd choose capris over shorts."

He snorted at her joke, but he wasn't about to let the subject of his picking her up at her home pass. Her refusal of his offer brought out some latent machismo, so he pressed the issue. "I don't mind swinging by to get you."

"I don't want my parents to know I'm looking into this."

Her blunt statement shut him down quite effectively. She didn't want her father to know she was keeping company with him. He couldn't blame her. He'd dealt with enough Henry Masters types to be sure his daughter slumming with a civil servant would stir the man's ire.

And he was all too aware of the strikes against him in the rest of the townspeople's eyes. He was an outsider. An outsider with mixed blood and an excess amount of melanin. A former federal agent to boot. There weren't too many families in Masters or Prescott County who had escaped the agency's dragnet unscathed.

They wanted him here for the same reasons they

found him lacking. After the upheaval caused by the DEA raids and adjacent charges, only someone with an unbiased eye and an indisputable reputation could set things to rights. Ben didn't mind being the outsider. He'd never fit in anywhere until he'd joined the agency, and look where he was now. Back on the outside looking in.

"Fine. We'll meet here at five thirty."

She nodded. "Thank you, Sheriff."

"You're welcome, Ms. Masters," he said, slipping back into the formalities as she had.

Without another word, she headed for the door. He watched, admiring the sway of her hips in her slim skirt and imagining the silky feel of her blouse under his fingertips. Because, no matter what their packaging, she was still a beautiful, intriguing woman, and he was undoubtedly a red-blooded man.

Chapter Eight

Ben went back to his place to change as well. Though the jeans and polo shirt weren't any more or less revealing than his uniform, he didn't want to be wearing a badge when he went poking holes in Marlee's theories. She obviously had her hopes pinned on uncovering something at the family's lake house.

When he pulled into the small parking lot adjacent to the municipal building, he spotted her right away. She had chosen cropped pants over shorts, but he couldn't be too disappointed. Though covered in utility pockets and made out of what looked to be parachute sheeting, they fit her perfectly. As did the simple white tank top she'd paired them with.

She stood in a sliver of shade provided by the angle of the sinking sun. For a moment, he wondered if she was hiding so no one would see her meeting up with him. Then he saw her smooth one of the tendrils of hair back up her neck and toward the ponytail she'd fashioned high atop her head. Hot. She was hot. In more ways than one.

The late-afternoon sun baked the cracked cement.

Heat rose off the unsheltered pavement in shimmering waves. Drawing to a halt right beside her, he kicked the air-conditioning in the SUV up a notch, then reached for the door handle. He was about to climb out when she yanked open the door and threw herself into the seat.

"Holy Moses, it's hot out there," she complained. Without asking, she reached over and switched the knob to force maximum airflow through the vents. "Air. I need air."

Amused, he drew his leg back in and closed his door again. "I was going to open the door for you."

She snorted, holding up a hand to stave off any other inane offers of assistance he might have offered, and leaned in to let the vent blow directly on her forehead. "Thanks, but I can manage myself."

"So I see." He twisted in his seat to swing an arm over the console. She didn't flinch away, but her movements stilled, like those of an animal scenting the air for danger. "I keep a cooler with some bottled water in here," he explained.

She relaxed visibly as he popped the lid on the plastic ice chest, and he forced himself not to be offended. After all, she was a woman alone in a car with a man who was a virtual stranger. She had every reason and right to be on her guard.

"Here." He wiped the bottom of the dripping bottle on the front of his shirt, then offered it to her. "It's pretty much tepid now, but…"

"Thank you," she said, taking the bottle.

He tried to keep his eyes to himself as she uncapped

it and took a long drink, but failed. She was so damn pretty. Not beautiful in the usual blonde Homecoming Queen way, but genuinely pretty. There were freckles on her nose and laugh lines forming at the corners of her eyes. Her hair looked soft and bouncy. He curled his hands into fists on his lap to keep from taking a playful swipe at her ponytail.

Marlee's eyes met his as she lowered the bottle. "What?"

"You should have let me pick you up," he chided gently.

"It's just…" She stopped, clearly torn over explaining. "My mother. She tends to be high-strung, and we're smack dab in the middle of cocktail hour. I didn't want to play twenty questions, so I sort of slipped out of the house."

"I've met your mother."

She shifted to look at him, but Ben thought it best not to reciprocate. He was particularly glad he hadn't when she said, "Then you are aware she's under the influence of…something most of the time. Don't worry. Daddy took the car keys away some time ago." Her voice was sad and wistful. "She never goes anywhere these days anyway."

"Your mother strikes me as a nice lady struggling with her grief."

"Who doesn't?" she said, her half smile self-deprecating. She settled into the seat then let out a huff of oxygen she must have been saving in case of emergency. "I haven't been out there." Apparently, he didn't respond quickly enough to the confession, because she clarified, "To the cabin. It was never my thing, and, well, after..."

"Your family used to own all the land around the lake, right?"

She whipped her head around so fast, her ponytail smacked the passenger window. "How did you find that out?"

He glanced over at her, then refocused on the narrow county road. "It came up in the investigation," he said with a shrug. "Was it a secret?"

"I guess not," she conceded the point grudgingly, then added, "More a surprise. At least for me."

He chanced another look at her. "You weren't aware your father owned the land?"

"No. I knew we owned it." She hesitated, then admitted, "I wasn't aware he'd sold it."

"The other parcels are owned by the Masters County Sportsmen's Club," he informed her.

"Whoever that is," she said peevishly.

She was clearly nettled by not being the only person with the facts at hand. Ben suspected if he let her steer the conversation her way, he might learn something new. "You aren't sure who's behind it?" He was curious to see how much she'd discovered and if she'd share her information with him.

"I guess it was my father's new general manager's idea."

He could feel her watching him closely, and he had to admit, a beautiful woman's scrutiny wasn't entirely unwelcome, regardless of the circumstances. He hadn't dated anyone since walking away from Atlanta with his life and a few haphazardly packed boxes.

"I gather there was quite a bit of...economic fall-out after the federal agencies made their presence in the area known."

Her careful wording added fuel to the pride he felt in playing a role in such a successful mission. It beat the tar out of the times when everything went belly-up. "We came short of firebombing the area to flush them out."

"Yes," she said, lifting a hand to indicate the approaching turnoff for the lake. He gave a brusque nod, and she let her hand fall. "I'm sorry. I guess you've been out here." She laced her fingers together in her lap.

"A couple times," he said. "I can get to the lake road, but I may need you to tell me how to get to your place."

"You were at the Youngs' the night they found Clint," she said quietly.

He dipped his head but kept his mouth shut.

"Used to be only our house and the Youngs' out here," she explained. "Follow the lake road about a quarter mile past their place, and you'll see our driveway."

He nodded. "So, your father sold these parcels off to cover real estate expenses?" he prompted, guiding her back on topic as he maneuvered the winding country road that roughly followed the same path as the lake's shoreline.

"Yes. Or so Wendell says," she answered with a shrug. "Seems like swatting a fly with a sledgehammer, but I guess there were costs beyond the actual cleaning and remediation."

"Lost rents and all," he concurred. He fed her a morsel of information in hopes of gaining more. "There were a number of Timber Masters employees involved. I imagine the repercussions went beyond the loss of the current tenants. They may have had a hard time finding new people to move in, given everyone found out what was happening in those houses."

"And my father rents the houses to people who work for the company directly," she added.

Ben bit his lips to keep from smiling. She'd inadvertently confirmed a point Timber Masters's attorneys had danced around in every single interview. There was nothing illegal about choosing to rent to a specific group of people, but there certainly was an issue if they refused to lease a property because they didn't belong to the group. Had pleasant, easygoing old Wendell Wingate been covering for a client who stepped over the line?

But he and Marlee Masters were on the same side of whatever it was they were doing now, he reminded himself sternly. He glanced away from the road as they passed the Youngs' driveway. He caught glimpses of the shake-shingled house through the trees, then drew a deep breath as he refocused on the road ahead of them.

As a member of the law enforcement community, he was so used to viewing lawyers with a jaundiced eye. Marlee had wanted him to come with her to her family's cabin in hopes of uncovering more of the mystery surrounding her brother's untimely death. Nothing more, nothing less.

"Were you close with your brother?"

His question seemed to startle her at first, but she recovered with a short laugh. "I keep forgetting you aren't from around here."

He kept his gaze on the faded yellow lines dividing the two-lane road. "Are you saying yes or no?"

"It's a yes," she said, amusement glinting in her eyes. "We were close." When he darted a look in her direction, she gave a helpless shrug. "I'm sorry. It's only... I got that question pretty often in Atlanta, but I never expected to hear it here in Pine Bluff." She sobered and pointed to a strip of reflectors marking an otherwise-unremarkable lane. "Go left up there."

He did. The *ticktock* of the blinker sounded extra loud in the silence of the car.

"We were close," she said as they started down the winding lane. "All our lives." Her voice caught on the last word. He peered at her, but she was dry-eyed. She motioned for him to pick up the pace again. "I find in families like ours, the kids either band together or go for one another's throats."

"How do you see your family?"

"It's more about how others see us. Families with money, property and some kind of perceived prestige," she said bluntly. "There are the expectations that come with those things."

The road widened as they went around another bend. He nearly swore when the rustic mansion she called a cabin came into view. Letting his foot off the gas, he let the SUV coast into the small gravel parking area. Shifting into Park, he asked, "You think your family's prestige is only perceived?"

"I think prestige is an external value," she said without missing a beat.

"Meaning?"

"It's an arbitrary value placed on someone or something based solely on someone else's say-so."

"I wouldn't say the clout your father wields around here is arbitrary," he countered.

"No, his is real, but it's different. It's power, not prestige," she asserted. "But my mother? Jeff? Me?" She shook her head. "We don't have any real power. We have prestige because other people perceive us as having power by proximity."

"'Power by proximity,'" he repeated.

"It's essentially a marketing tactic," she continued. "I'm not saying I didn't make the most of it back in high school," she admitted, "but Jeff and I...we had no illusions about who holds the power."

He blinked, surprised by her candor. "I see."

"Anyhow, I'm talking too much. I have no idea why I told you all that. We should go in."

But rather than bailing out of the car, Marlee gazed pensively through the windshield. Needing to move past the moment, he threw his shoulder against the door as he opened it. She hadn't stirred by the time he reached the passenger door, so he grabbed the handle and swung it open wide. Marlee's eyebrows rose, and she blinked those big blue eyes.

He glanced down at the ground to see if he'd parked in a puddle or something. "What?"

"You aren't going to offer your hand? What if I injure myself stepping down from here? I might twist an ankle on the gravel or something."

The urge to reach in and haul her out of the truck by her waist was strong, but he restrained himself. She could play semantics with "prestige" and "power," but he couldn't gamble his job on the belief that her goading was playful. After all, she'd admitted to using her position as a Masters once upon a time. What if this whole trip out to the lake was nothing more than some kind of trap?

"I've got this."

He followed her up the natural-stone pathway, mentally kicking himself. Jogging a couple steps to match her long, irritated stride, he huffed in frustration—which seemed to be his primary state around this woman. "Listen, you said yourself your father's power isn't a matter of perception. Who do you think hired me?"

"My father hired you," she said without bothering to look at him.

"And he can fire me."

"I'm not going to get you fired." She paused and heaved a heavy sigh when they reached the bottom of the porch steps. Then she looked up at him, her expression earnest. "Look, I think I just wanted someone to be here with me, and for some reason, you were the person I thought of." She bit her lip, then gave a barely there shrug. "Maybe because you're the sheriff but mostly because I wanted someone…objective to talk things through."

"Maybe you should try talking to your dad."

His cautious response seemed to trip some kind of trigger in her. She spun away from him and headed for the door. "My father and I don't have a relationship conducive to conversation. It's more along the lines of he gives orders, and I do my best to ignore them until I have no other choice."

He laughed. "Is that how he got you back here? He made it so you had no other choice?"

"Essentially." She stooped and flipped back the corner of a welcome mat featuring the Timber Masters logo. "He's good at getting his way." Holding a key, she sprang up with a grin and an eye roll. "See? Typical Henry. He simply assumes no one would dare break into his house, and guess what? He's right most of the time."

"You're a grown woman. An attorney." He heard the click of tumblers in the lock, and the back of his neck itched. He was there with a legitimate invitation, but instinct had him checking over his shoulder anyway. "I understand you're starting out, fresh from school and all, but surely you could have found some way to keep living life on your own terms."

She stiffened, then said only, "You'd think, right?"

Marlee gave the knob a twist and peered inside, but Ben saw the flash of raw vulnerability streak across her beautiful face. If he drew attention to it, she'd cover it up, so he remained silent as he took in the details of the setting. The trim around the windows had been painted fairly recently. He'd bet the cream-colored enamel hadn't had a full year of weathering. The oak-and-glass door swung on well-oiled hinges. Marlee groped for the light switch, then gasped as the dim interior of the house went from murky and dark to high definition.

Her hand flew to her mouth, and there was no way he could refrain from placing a steadying hand on her shoulder. "Easy. You don't have to go in there."

She turned away from the entry and stalked across the porch. Bracing both hands on the rough-hewn rail, she let her head fall forward as she drew in shuddering breaths.

Ben hung back, giving the interior of the cabin a quick once-over while he had the chance. High-end appliances. The main room was clearly styled to appeal to an outdoorsman but in a tasteful way. No tacky fake fish or mass-produced man cave gewgaws. It was filled with warm neutral colors, textured fabrics thrown about on soft leather furniture and a big, sturdy coffee table with an array of hunting and fishing books and magazines. But where it should have felt homey and comfortable, it fell shy of the mark. Deliberately casual, Ben decided. He would say one thing for Henry Masters—he took good care of his property. Too bad he seemed to be so careless of his kin.

Without a word, he moved to stand next to her. When she shot him a look from under lowered lashes, he leaned in and planted his hands on the rail, mirroring her stance. It was a tactic used in negotiations. And mating rituals. Ben didn't allow himself to dwell on which he thought he was doing. He couldn't, not when the woman beside him was staring intently out at the lake, blinking back tears.

"I'm sorry. The memories must be—"

Marlee twisted to face him, her piercing stare locking on his profile and stopping his attempt at establishing empathy dead in its tracks.

"You don't get it. There are no memories in there. It's been gutted." Her voice was low and quavering, but he didn't have to be a shrink to recognize the source. She wasn't sad—she was angry.

"Excuse me?"

"The whole place. It's totally different. Hell, some of the walls are even gone." A fat tear trickled past her lashes, and she swiped at it with the inside of her wrist. "It's, uh…a whole new house. Like it never happened."

Two more tears followed, and Ben had to tighten his grip on the railing to keep from reaching for her, pulling her into his arms and kissing them away. He looked her in the eye, forcing himself to dig his fingers into the rail and keep his voice even as he replied, "But it did happen."

"Yes."

Her voice broke on the single syllable, and she gazed out at the lake again. He followed her lead. Minutes passed with nothing but the sound of birdcalls and buzzing bees. He heard her draw in a deep breath. The air around them shifted, and Ben could have sworn he felt the planks beneath his feet move too.

"Maybe a complete overhaul was the point of the renovation."

She rolled her shoulders back and looked him in the eye. "My brother didn't kill himself."

She spoke with such quiet conviction, he wanted to believe her, but the evidence—

Marlee interrupted the thought. "He didn't. Except I have no way to prove it."

Straightening away from the rail, he settled his hands on his hips. "There's not one shred of evidence in either case pointing to anything else."

Marlee crossed her arms over her chest, tipped her chin up a notch and stared him down. "He didn't do it."

"Marlee—"

"I know!" she snapped. Forcing herself to settle, she gestured to the lake. "Something about the sale of this property stinks," she continued. He opened his mouth, but she raised a hand to stop him. "Name. Duty. Legacy," she said, counting each word off on her fingers, then holding them high for him to see. "Henry Masters doesn't give up what's his. Certainly not property the family has owned for generations."

Ben nodded, encouraging her to get it all out, even though he believed her suppositions to be wildly baseless. She obviously needed to talk her theories through with someone. Might as well be him.

"The timber around Sawtooth Lake seeded the Timber Masters empire. My great-great-great-grandfather learned the logging trade here on this land as a way of earning his way out of debt." Her chin thrust out, she shifted her gaze to the lake again, blinking furiously. Setting her jaw, she shook her head in sad dismissal. "You see? There was no piece of property in the world that meant as much to my father as these acres. I can't imagine him allowing them to be sold."

"But he did sell them," Ben reminded her gently.

She shook her head again, but this time, her confusion was written all over her beautiful face. "My brother was the one who wanted to sell."

He scowled as he mulled the information over. "Even so, wouldn't your father have had to sign the papers?"

Marlee shrugged. "My father did sign the papers but not until after Jeff died."

"Why then?"

"'Why then?' is the big question."

"Maybe he wanted to follow through on one of your brother's plans?"

"If my father had one ounce of sentimentality, I'd say maybe, but he doesn't. It would take a lot more than some construction costs and lost rents for my father to agree to selling this particular property. There was something else going on, and I'm determined to get to the bottom of it."

"And you want my help," he concluded flatly.

"I *need* your help," she corrected.

Ben blinked, surprised by the blunt admission. Marlee Masters struck him as the sort of woman who prided herself on not needing anyone—which made her request almost irresistible. But not completely. He'd been run out of Atlanta and lost the job he'd once loved. Pine Bluff was supposed to be a respite. A place where he could rest, recuperate and figure out what he was going to do with the rest of his life after his twenty-year plan had been blown to bits. If he crossed swords with Henry Masters, where would he go from there?

Still, he couldn't help wondering what roiled beneath the surface in his new hometown. Here was Marlee Masters herself, giving him an engraved invitation to poke around. "Fine. I'm in. Where do we start?"

Chapter Nine

Marlee gave him a moment to ruminate on whatever it was holding him back, then she placed a hand on his arm to pull him back into the conversation. This time, he was the one to drag both their gazes down to the fingers curled around his bicep.

"Thank you," she said softly.

"You're welcome."

When she didn't withdraw her hand, Ben's heart gave a hard thud. A bad thud. The kind of thud that said, "This way lies danger." Forcing himself to take a step back, he tried not to let the regret he felt when her touch slid away take hold. He couldn't afford to get tangled up with a woman like Marlee Masters.

He cleared his throat. "Listen, uh, I came here to do a job, and I think it's best if I do that job without complications."

The stiff declaration actually startled a laugh out of her. "Are you kidding? You think you can move to a town this small, declare yourself the law and expect to live your life without anyone trying to complicate it?" She scoffed. "You must be a city guy. Small towns don't work the same way."

"You're right. I am a city guy. But I don't care how it works because this may not be a long-term solution for me."

He stopped speaking abruptly. His eyes widened. Whatever he meant, it was a revelation. And one she should probably get a handle on. Trying for cool and unruffled, she forced the corners of her mouth up. This time, she bent over farther, letting her forearms rest atop the smooth wood of the rail, and she squinted at the late-afternoon sun glinting off the water.

"Not a long-term solution," she repeated. "Interesting. I don't suppose you mentioned the bit about Pine Bluff being a pit stop in your job interview?"

"I never said it was a pit stop," he countered.

"But you're not here for the long-term, are you?"

"I want something more permanent but…maybe not here. Are you staying?"

She'd touched a nerve with the sheriff, but she didn't feel obliged to answer his question. Instead, she parried. "How does a big-time federal agent end up getting himself banished to the backwoods anyway?"

"I wasn't banished. I applied for the job."

His attempt to play semantics with her were of no consequence. "You applied and bamboozled my father with your big shotery, I bet."

Her phrasing broke some of the tension. Ben let out a short bark of laughter then bent down to mimic her position. "I'm not sure exactly what big shotery involves, but I can tell you I've never bamboozled anyone."

She'd buy that. This guy was textbook cop. All rugged self-assurance with a side of truth and justice for all thrown in. She smirked at the large man folded nearly in half beside her. She recognized the move for what it was. They'd learned about the psychology behind body language in law school too. No matter how good he looked doing it, no amount of mirroring would make her trust him. Yet. Besides, he was the one on the defensive, and she was the one who had put him there. She needed to move past how insanely attractive she found him and go in for the kill.

"Who did you have to fool to get the job?"

"I wasn't fooling anyone, and from what I hear, the hiring committee was unanimous in its decision."

"The hiring committee comprised of my father and…" She made a circular motion, encouraging him to expound.

"Your father, Wendell Wingate and the county prosecutor, Duane Wade," he said helpfully. "Who, I can assure you, did not live up to the expectations the name might inspire."

The last part threw her off. "What expectations were those?"

He raised a hand to indicate someone who only came up to his shoulder in height. "Little guy. Bet he doesn't break five-ten on a good day."

"Yes, I've met Duane, but what does his height have to do with anything? He's a heck of a prosecutor."

"You don't know who Dwyane Wade is? The NBA player?" he prompted.

Tickled by his obvious impatience, she widened her

eyes. "Oh, you mean basketball?" When he snorted a laugh, she chuckled along with him. "Did you actually think you were going to have some all-star athlete interview you to be sheriff in Podunk, Georgia?"

He shrugged. "A guy can hope."

They laughed together, but her laughter quickly faded when the dusk-to-dawn porch light came on. Marlee groaned when she saw they'd left the door to the house wide-open and the lights on. Wouldn't her father love to find his newly renovated lake house infested with mosquitoes?

"Coming out here was a bad idea," she admitted, then pushed from the rail. She stalked over to the door to switch off the lights and lock the place up again. Once she placed the key back under the mat, she brushed her hands together, dusting off the notion of returning to the scene of the…scene.

They walked back to his SUV side by side. She could feel the warmth radiating from him. The fine hairs on her arms stood on end as they navigated the uneven foot path, but still, they didn't touch. When they reached the passenger side of the car, he reached for the door handle and swung it open wide. She stepped around him to enter but drew up short when he thrust out his hand.

She blushed as she placed the tips of her fingers in his open palm. "Why, thank you, kind sir," she cooed as she stepped up into the cab. He closed his fingers, gripping hers firmly, and Marlee sobered as she tried to get a read on his expression. "What?"

"You are exactly the kind of woman I can't risk,"

he said gruffly. Taken aback by the vehemence in his words, she tried to pull her hand from his, but he held fast. "Women like you…"

He kept squeezing her fingers, but he didn't finish his sentence. She narrowed her eyes. "Women like me, what?"

"You can only be trouble for a man like me," he answered without hesitation or even the slightest hint of remorse. "We come from different worlds."

"I don't recall asking you to do anything—"

"You didn't have to ask," he interrupted. "You with your beauty-queen smiles and steel trap of a mind. You're tuned in to exactly how powerful you are. You use it. You were born knowing how to use it."

She yanked her hand from his, wincing when her elbow jammed into her rib cage. "You think you can read me how?"

"Because I know someone just like you," he said, still crowding the open door. "Or, I should say, I know *of* one."

Despite her irritation, she couldn't help rising to the bait. "Only one? To hear you talk, you'd think we were pretty thick on the ground. Surely you should have more than one former beauty queen under your belt."

"I don't have any under my belt," he said, practically snarling the last words at her.

"But you said you knew one—"

"She was my mother," he said in a growl. Then he stepped back and slammed the car door. The problem was, she wasn't clear if he meant it as a period or an exclamation point.

THEY HARDLY SPOKE to one another as they made their way back into town. Marlee stared out the passenger window, unseeing but seething inside. How dare he presume to understand her? How dare he think he could lump her in with other women? He didn't know the first thing about her, what she was capable of or what she wanted out of life. She was the daughter of the man who ran this tiny town. Everything else he thought he knew about her was pure presumption.

It galled her that he assumed he had her number. What had he meant about his mother? What could she have to do with anything? And how could she have been thinking about kissing a man who was clearly comparing her to his mother? Had her instincts gone completely haywire?

She was still fuming when he pulled to a stop in front of her parents' home. He pressed the brake so hard, the car rocked forward and then back, jolting her from her thoughts. She gaped up at the house looming in the deepening dusk. The windows were ablaze with lights. Her father's enormous car sat parked in the drive rather than pulled into the carriage house beyond the main residence. Heaven forbid the man not be able to make a quick getaway.

Crap. Her father was home, and she was being delivered to the front walk in the sheriff's car. She glanced over at Mrs. Plunkett's house and saw a lace curtain drop back into place. A hot flush of irritation mixed with mortification crept up her neck. By now, everyone who lived in the big old houses lining the block had seen them.

"What are you doing? Why did you bring me here?" she demanded.

"This is where you live, isn't it?" He unfurled his fingers from the steering wheel long enough to gesture to the brick-and-stone mansion built by her great-grandfather.

"Yes, but," she sputtered, "I met you at the station for a reason."

He leveled her with a flat stare. "I'm sorry if you're embarrassed to be seen with me, Marlee, but it's growing dark, and even small towns have their creepers."

Their gazes locked. "Speaking of creepers, he was quiet today." She pulled her phone from one of the pockets of her capris, then scowled when she saw she had five unread messages. She'd forgotten to unmute her notifications after she'd left the office. "Or not," she said, tapping to open the app.

The first message was from her mother wanting her to be home for dinner. Marlee cringed. She hated to worry or inconvenience her mother. It only led to closer scrutiny. She'd simply forgotten how to live under her parents' thumbs. She'd been excited to see Ben, she admitted—only to herself. She pushed aside the morass of mixed feelings and focused on the screen. The four others were from unknown numbers.

"He texted," Ben said flatly.

"I silenced everything when I got to work this morning. I didn't want to give my father any excuse to start in on his 'cell phones are the scourge of man' rant on my first day."

Leaning into the console, she angled the screen so he could see too. The first message read only:

The skirt is good but last nights outfit was better

The next came from an entirely different area code.

Business barbie walking down the street in your sexy shoes sipping your milkshake

She sucked in a sharp breath, wondering how close her stalker had actually gotten to her. She had her answer when she tapped open the next message:

You should be choosier about the company you keep

The last read simply:

Your daddy know you and ben kinsella go out to his lake house to screw around

Ben emitted a low growling sound as he read the last one. Marlee couldn't help wondering if he was more perturbed by the invasion or the insinuation.

"He's too close," Ben said at last. "You need to tell your father about these messages."

"Oh, no," she said with a harsh laugh. "No way."

"Marlee, this guy could be hiding out in your bushes right now," he said heatedly. "This town is small, and Lord knows it seems impossible for you to go unnoticed, but in this case, proximity doesn't mean you're safe."

The residual heat from her embarrassment morphed into a blush of pleasure. Still, telling her father was out of the question. Reaching over, she placed a gentling hand on his thigh. "Ben, I get that you mean well, but telling my father is not a good option. First, he'd insist I bring this to you, which I already have done. Second, I'm not exactly sure who all was involved in this deal with the Sportsmen's Club, but it wouldn't have happened without my father's signing off on the idea. I don't want to show my hand until I can figure out what stinks about it."

He jabbed a finger at her phone. "But this guy isn't talking about the club, or the property, or even your brother. His focus is all on you."

"I understand." She lifted the hand off his leg. "That's why this is my business. Sharing these messages with you or my father or anyone at all is completely my choice. I chose you," she said pointedly. "And Lori," she added after a beat. "I took this directly to my local law enforcement officers for a reason. I am an adult. What my father needs to know about my life is something I decide, not you."

They stared one another down for a moment.

"I want you to be safe," he grumbled at last.

"I appreciate your concern." She lowered her hand again, and this time treated herself to giving his hard, muscled thigh a friendly pat. "In the future, I would appreciate it if you didn't drop me off in front of my house in a marked vehicle for God and all the neighbors to see."

His lips thinned into a line. "I didn't realize you were ashamed to be seen with me."

"I'm not. But all the same, I don't need the ladies at bridge club asking my mother if I got caught shoplifting penny candy from the drugstore again."

The admission coaxed a deep chuckle from him. "'Again'?"

"I was seven, and believe me, I paid for my crime."

His self-deprecating grin set her heart aflutter. "It's a good thing juvenile records are sealed. You might not have passed the background check for the bar."

She caught a movement on the porch and saw her father standing there waiting for her, his hands on his hips. "Oh, boy."

Ben blew out a breath, then said a soft, "Sorry."

She shook her head as she reached for the door handle. "No. It's no problem. If there's one thing I excel at, it's handling my daddy." She hesitated for a moment, then opened the door. Her voice softened as she stepped out of the SUV. "Thanks for going out there with me, Ben."

"It was my pleasure."

Something about the way he said the last word made warmth gather low in her belly. "I'll talk to you tomorrow."

"Hey," he called out to her. "Call me if you hear anything else from your texter."

She nodded. "I will." Then, raising her voice, she said, "Thanks for the lift home, Sheriff. I'll be sure to send a check to the widows-and-orphans fund."

Marlee caught a snatch of his laughter as the heavy

door thunked between them. She made her way up the front walk and greeted her father with studied casualness. "Hey, Daddy."

He jerked a chin toward the taillights on Ben's vehicle. "What was that about?"

"What was—" Marlee looked over her shoulder as if she hadn't given a second thought as to how she came to be there. "Oh, he gave me a ride home. I was talking to Lori about Jeff and didn't realize how dark it was."

Her father's expression morphed from suspicious to grim to obvious discomfiture all in the blink of an eye. "Oh."

He couldn't and wouldn't say much more because Marlee had hit on the two topics of conversation her father avoided as much as humanly possible—his lost son and Jeff's relationship with the "Cabrera girl." He hadn't approved of their relationship and made no secret of his opinions.

"Your mother was worried," he admonished as she sauntered past him, determined to reach the safety of her room without too many questions.

Her steps faltered when she crossed the threshold. Guilt plucked at the string of tension in her gut. She glanced back to find her father staring at his own vehicle, stark longing etched into his once-handsome features. For a split second, she felt sorry for him. His only son was gone, and he was losing his wife to pills and alcohol because he couldn't find it in him to share in her grief. But, as quickly as the sympathy flared in her, it died. Smothered by the recollection of how he'd passed her off to Wendell Wingate on her first day.

"I'm heading up. I'll tell Mama I'm sorry about dinner. I guess I'm not used to checking in with anyone."

"Yeah, well, you're not off running wild all around Atlanta anymore," he chided, stepping inside and closing the door behind them. "Around here, people will notice where you are and what you're doing."

She paused at the foot of the ornately carved staircase, her hand tightening on the newel post as she looked back over her shoulder. "Don't forget to add 'who I'm with' to the list."

"That's a given," he said darkly, clearly unamused by her sass.

"Well, you can rest assured I've only been spending time with the esteemed members of our local law enforcement and legal communities today," she said as she started up the stairs, her pace unhurried. It was a tiny show of defiance, but when one was playing on Henry Masters's turf, one took every victory they could get.

At the landing, Marlee glanced back to find her father watching her, a vertical line bisecting his brows. She forced herself to keep to the same measured pace until she gained the top of the stairs. There, she made a beeline for her mother's suite of rooms. Outside Carolee's door, she took a moment to calm her breathing, then pressed an ear to the door. Neither screams nor sobs greeted her. Marlee took the quiet as a good sign. Tapping lightly with her fingernails, she twisted the knob and opened the door an inch or so.

"Mama?"

"That you, Marlee baby?" her mother called from

the love seat situated in front of a large flat-screen television. Carolee clasped a tumbler of clear liquid in one hand and the remote control in the other. "You eat somethin'?"

Marlee could tell by the laid-back slur her mother was already well into the evening's allotment of vodka, so she didn't step farther into the room. "I did, Mama."

"You wanna watch *The Matchmaker* with me, sugar?"

Marlee repressed a shudder at the thought of being trapped on Carolee's settee being force-fed trash TV. "Not tonight, Mama. I'm wiped out."

"Sleep well, sugar," her mother called, her attention riveted to the screen.

Marlee smirked as she pulled the door closed. Her mother didn't seem to think there was anything strange about a twenty-five-year-old woman claiming exhaustion at eight in the evening.

In her room, Marlee walked directly to the window, closed the slats and dropped the sheer curtains into place over them. Only then did she switch on the light. Seconds later, her phone buzzed.

Spoilsport.

She made an unladylike hand gesture toward the window, hoping her Peeping Tom might have hung around for the shadow-puppet show.

Chapter Ten

Ben hated to admit it, but he'd spent the better part of the next day hoping to run into her. No such luck. He'd seen her from a distance, though. She'd been driving her father's mammoth SUV rather than her own car, and her mother had been in the passenger seat. He'd whiled away the rest of the day assuming she was tied up with family business. Expectations adjusted, he'd been pleasantly surprised when her name and number appeared on his phone. "Hello?"

"You busy?" Marlee asked without preamble.

He muted his television. "No."

"I can tell you whoever my creeper is, he has a pretty good view of my window," she said grimly.

Stomach knotting, Ben flexed his free hand to keep from balling up a fist. "He texted you?"

She blew out a long, gusty breath. "Yes."

"And you're only telling me now?"

"Yes, because I handled it," she said with exaggerated patience.

"How? How did you handle it?"

"I closed the blinds and drew the curtains."

"But he texted you."

"Yes."

Ben squeezed his eyes shut, quickly tiring of their game of twenty questions. "What did it say?"

A moment later, a text came through. Spoilsport.

Something live and primal growled deep inside him, but Ben bit his tongue. He couldn't give vent to his own fear and anger. His job here was to alleviate hers. "So," he said, keeping his tone neutral, "did he text anything else?"

"Not yet," she admitted.

He ran the flat of his palm over his face. "Do you think he's out there tonight?"

"Do you want me to go out and look?"

The sarcasm behind the question came through loud and clear. "No. I—" He clamped his mouth shut. He was babbling inanities because he couldn't run right over there, yank this bastard out of whatever bush he was hiding in and beat him to a pulp. "I'll call Mike and ask him to spend some extra time patrolling the area."

"I'd appreciate that," she said at last.

"And Marlee?"

"Yeah?"

"It sounds more a game to him. He's scary and annoying, but he doesn't seem to be escalating." He closed his eyes, hoping he was right and not simply fooling the both of them in his attempt to soothe her.

"Right," she said after a beat.

"He wants to rattle you, but I don't think he wants to hurt you." At least, he prayed his instincts were right on this point. A beep sounded in his ear, and he pulled the phone away to see who was calling on the other line. "Oh, hey, Mike is calling. I'll ask him to step up his circuits around your house. You try to get some rest."

"Got it, Officer."

He exhaled, glad to hear some of her sass back. "I'll talk to you later."

He flashed over to Mike. "Hey, what's up?"

"Ben?" the young deputy managed to croak. Dread slithered down Ben's spine as he listened to Mike's labored breathing on the other end of the line.

"What? What is it?" he demanded.

"I was listening to the scanner earlier, and I heard some of the guys from Prescott County going back and forth concerning a possible 10-56."

Ben sucked in a breath. In all his years as an agent, he'd never had reason to hear the code called. Now, he'd heard it twice in as many weeks. He cringed as he caught on to the one dim bright spot Mike had offered. They wouldn't be handling this case. Whoever the poor victim was, they'd be Prescott County's headache. Still, their jurisdiction overlapped in so many areas, the departments shared a close working relationship.

Exhaling loudly, he scrubbed his right eye with the heel of his hand. "Man, this is rough. Who's on the case?"

"Watson and Rainey," Mike reported. "But that's not the kicker."

Ben lowered his hand, then gripped the arm of the couch to brace himself against what he feared may be a cyclone heading his way. "Let me hear it."

"No ID on the body. The Prescott guys don't recognize him. They want us to come over to see if we can get a visual."

Ben groaned, letting his forehead drop into his palm. He hadn't lived there long enough to give a positive identification on more than a dozen people, tops. Which meant he and one of his deputies had to go and look at another dead body. Then and there, he decided to take Lori. She was made of tough stuff, and Mike was still shaken from seeing Clint Young's body.

"Do they think he's local?"

"Yes. They found him in a half-built house. One of those fancy architectural places…" Mike took a deep breath, then let it out in a rush. "Out on Sawtooth Lake."

SHE CAUGHT HERSELF holding her phone long after Ben had ended the call. Embarrassed, even though there was no one around to witness her moment of girliness, she tossed it onto the bed and strolled into her bathroom. There, she stripped off her clothes and dropped them onto the floor as she waited for the water in the shower to warm.

Earlier in the evening, she'd driven her mother to a committee meeting at Trudy Skyler's house. She'd sat and dutifully sipped iced tea while the women dithered over what kind of Christmas decorations to order for the town's lampposts. Mostly, she'd thought about Ben and how annoyed she'd been with Wendell for keeping her so busy that she hadn't had a chance to slip over to the municipal building to "drop in" on him. After an evening of screeching, bickering and incessant gossip, Marlee had only wanted to hear his smooth, deep voice.

Holding her hand under the tap to test the water temperature, she hummed softly as she took in her surroundings. The bathroom fittings were old enough to be considered retro. The walls were covered in white-on-white tiles but not the elongated subway-style one saw on all the home-decor shows. Still, the ceramic surfaces gleamed.

She'd missed the old claw-foot tub when she moved away. Her parents had updated it with a rainwater showerhead and charming circular shower curtain, but when she was younger, she'd preferred baths to showers. There were countless evenings when she'd lounge in the tub until the water cooled, reading a book or listening to music.

Only the years of dormitory living as an undergrad and frenetic pace of law school broke her of the habit. She'd grown accustomed to taking nothing more than the necessary five minutes to scrub herself clean and wash her hair. Now, she was home again and not working the sixty-hour weeks most first-year law associates work. She'd have to learn to downshift, take long soaks again. As she drew back the curtain and stepped over the high side of the tub, she made a mental note to pick up some scented bath salts.

Five minutes later, she had a chamois hair towel twisted around her head and a thick bath sheet—one of the ones her mother's housekeeper, Mrs. Franklin, laundered and sprayed with lavender water as they line dried in the sun—wrapped around her body. The long evening hours stretched in front of her. Marlee meticulously applied lotion to every inch of her still-damp skin in a vain attempt to distract herself from the restlessness roiling inside her. Unwinding the hair towel, she finger-combed her hair into wet waves, content to let it air-dry on this warm evening. The steam trapped in the tiled room threatened to make a second shower necessary, so she moved into the cool spaciousness of her bedroom to finish drying off. The house was air-conditioned but built in the days before modern insulation and ductwork. The system worked well enough when it came to sucking the humidity out of the air, but it never felt overly cool.

Holding the knot of the towel, she went straight to the dresser. Her feet skimmed across smooth wood floors. She looked forward to dropping the thick towel and slipping into the cool cotton of one of her brother's old shirts. Wresting a washed-thin Atlanta Braves tee from the bureau, she shook it out, then stopped dead in her tracks.

The sheer curtains had been pushed apart and the slats of the blinds cranked open.

The T-shirt whooshed to the floor at her feet. She blinked twice, unable to believe what she was seeing. But she wasn't imagining it. The slats were angled down. At precisely the correct angle for someone on the street below to see inside.

Clutching her towel tight, she bolted from the room and into the empty hall. She ran to the opposite side of the house, toward her parents' rooms, and skidded to a halt outside her mother's door. The muffled sound of the television leaked out into the hall, but Marlee heard no other noise. Twisting the knob silently, she opened the door enough to see her mother sprawled across the love seat fully dressed, out cold. She held her breath until she caught the rumble of a soft snore, then gently closed the door again.

Her mother wouldn't have been much good in this sort of situation anyway. Making her way to the top of the stairs, Marlee listened for sounds from the first floor. Nothing. Her father might have gone out. But then again, it was also possible she'd run into one of her father's cronies. They came and went at all hours. Usually, they carried important papers and claimed there was some form of business to be discussed, but mostly the men hung out on the back veranda and drank bourbon.

She hesitated, still gripping the oversize towel tightly to her chest. She should go back to her room and dress. She could grab her phone while she was there and…what? Call the sheriff and ask him to come look under her bed?

But she didn't want to go back to her room. Not until she figured out who'd been in there while she'd been in the shower. Grasping the banister with her free hand, she padded down the steps as quietly as century-old wood would allow. The front door was closed, but she'd lay odds it wasn't locked. Biting her lip, Marlee made her way toward the back of the house, pausing for a moment at the partially closed door to her father's study. Two men were talking. One was her father, but she didn't recognize the other man's voice. The last thing she could do was show up at the door to her father's study and expect him to introduce her to whoever it was while she was dressed in only a towel.

Moving as soundlessly as she could, she slipped past the study and tiptoed to the back of the house. The laundry was off the kitchen. She prayed Mrs. Franklin had left something she could slip into in the tiny closet of a room. When she saw the empty hampers and abandoned drying racks, she heaved a heavy sigh. Biting her lip as she gave the towel yet another mournful glance, she consoled herself with the knowledge she could sneak up the narrow back staircase from the kitchen without being seen. She was about to do so when she spotted the canvas bag full of dry cleaning ready to be taken to the cleaners.

"Oh, thank goodness," she said as she abandoned her hold on the towel and began rooting through the bag for something belonging to her. She spotted the black dress she'd worn to Clint Young's visitation and plunged her hand deeper into the bag. The towel came unfurled, but she didn't care. The sides gaped like loosened tent flaps as she shoved her arm into the bag nearly to her shoulder.

"Excuse me, ma'am? Are you all right?"

The question was drawled low. The timbre of his voice conveyed secrecy but failed to mask the speaker's amusement at the sight she must have presented. Yanking her arm from the dry-cleaning bag, she scrambled to get hold of both sides of the bath sheet as it slid another inch down her back. She tugged it all the way up into her armpits, knotted it and shifted the closure so she could pin it in place with her arm. Pushing her now-tangled hair back from her face, she straightened to her full height and faced the intruder head-on.

A tall man with the lithe, athletic build of a distance runner stood near the kitchen counter, clutching an unopened bottle of bourbon by its neck. His hair was golden blond and about a half inch too long to be considered well-kept. His skin was sun-kissed, and his teeth so white and even, she wondered for a moment if they were caps. She met his frank perusal with a once-over of her own.

"Who are you? And why are you in my kitchen?" She raised her chin a smidge in hopes of coming off more imperious than indecent.

"I'm Will Thomason," he said, brimming with confidence. "You must be Miss Marlee. I keep meanin' to come meet you, but we've been doing some reshuffling of personnel, what with Clint and all…"

The name registered with her, but Marlee wasn't in a giving mood at the moment. She was freaked out, mostly naked, and there was a strange man in her house.

"Have you been in my room?"

Sandy brows shot high. He made a bit of a production out of blinking once, then shook his head. Something about the way he never broke eye contact with her made her mistrust him. It was a tell, a gambit many people misplayed. Oddly enough, the fact that he didn't peek at any other part of her felt like an act of aggression. Was he daring her to question his integrity? If so, she would.

"Were you?"

"Was I in your room?" he parried, still locked in on her eyes.

"Yes."

"Why would I have been in your room? We've only just met." At last, he looked down at the bottle in his hand. "I only came in here to get a fresh bottle for your father. If you want to show me your room, I think we might be better off waiting until your parents aren't home," he said, dropping what she assumed he thought was a playful wink at her.

"It wasn't an invitation. It was a question," she stated through clenched teeth.

"Will, did you find it?"

Marlee closed her eyes and cringed as her father's footsteps rang out against the hardwood floors. "Right above the stove. I keep it up high so—" He stopped on a dime when he spotted her standing in the laundry room door wearing nothing but a towel. "Marlee? What the hell?"

"I think I walked in as Ms. Masters was looking for something in the laundry," Will said, flashing a charmingly sheepish smile at his employer, then her. "I'm afraid we startled each other."

"Why are you running around the house half-naked?" her father demanded.

"I was—" The temptation to use Will Thomason's cover story was tempting, but there was something off about him. She didn't want to give the man the chance to latch on to some kind of rescuer image of himself. "I was in the shower and someone came in my room."

Her father pulled his head back, puzzlement written all over his face. "In your room?"

"While I was taking a shower. Someone was in my room while I was taking a shower." Thankfully, her voice didn't fail her as she stared the two men down. "I came down to see who was in the house."

"You thought whoever it was might be hiding in the hamper?" Will asked, and she decided she loathed the dimple that flashed in his cheek when he chuckled at his own joke.

Now she was too annoyed to be mortified, which, in a way, made Marlee happy. Rolling her shoulders back, she repeated her question. "Was it you?"

"No." He held her gaze in his disconcerting way.

"Why would Will be in your bedroom?" her father demanded.

"I don't have the faintest idea," she said with exaggerated calm. "Why would anyone else be in my room?"

Her father shook his head dismissively. "No one was in your room. If there was anyone, it was your mother," he said. "I've been down here the whole time."

"When did he get here?" she pressed, waving a hand at Will Thomason.

"Will's been here all evening. We're working on an acquisition proposal," her father said impatiently. "He hasn't left my office."

"Except when I went out to my car to get my power cord for my laptop," Will supplied helpfully, a shade too jovial for her liking.

Henry huffed and waved his hand as if her concerns

were nothing more than a swarm of gnats. "Yes, well, that's neither here nor there."

"Or in Miss Marlee's room," Will added without missing a beat. He gazed at her, his expression all blank innocence. "Full disclosure, I believe I also availed myself to the powder room a time or two." He hefted the bottle of bourbon. "You see, I wasn't allowed anything more than water until I'd finished my homework."

"Enough," Henry said, annoyed with the disruption of his evening. "You two wanna flirt, do it on your own time."

The mere suggestion that this confrontation with a stranger in her home was a flirtation made Marlee's skin crawl. "We are not flirting."

"I believe Miss Marlee's tastes run more along the lines of the law enforcement type," Will said, his oh-so-casual drawl drawing the observation out to the point of pain.

"Don't be ridiculous," her father said, dismissing the notion out of hand, despite his earlier display of concern. "We have work to do. Marlee, go on back upstairs. You can't be running around here in nothing but a towel. What would your mother say?"

She wanted to tell him she wouldn't say a thing because she was too busy being passed out at eight in the evening, but her father had already lost interest. Henry snatched the bourbon bottle out of Will Thomason's hand, then gestured for the younger man to precede him.

Will inclined his head to her. "It was a pleasure to meet you." The polite sentiment didn't quite match the predatory gleam in his eyes. Thankfully, he followed her father out of the kitchen and back down the hall.

She crept out of the tiny space she'd backed into and stood for a moment, holding tight to the towel and listening to the low rumble of the two men's voices. Will said something about how pretty she was, and Marlee had to resist the urge to make gagging noises. Then she heard her father say something about how he should have introduced the two of them earlier and how he'd always hoped Will Thomason might "hit it off" with her, and the rough outline of her father's plan began to take shape.

Horrified, she bolted for the back stairs. Bare feet slapped the varnished wood of the upstairs hallway as she stomped her way back to her room. Muttering under her breath, she rushed in. She stuck close to the walls in an effort to avoid walking directly in front of the window, then scooped up the Braves shirt and her phone, retreating to the safety of her bathroom.

Heart pounding, she locked the door behind her and tapped the screen to call Ben. The second the call connected, she slumped against the door, her towel coming unraveled as she sank to the cool tile floor. "You will not believe what happened over here," she began without greeting.

The connection crackled, and she heard Ben speaking, but his words came across garbled.

Frustrated by the delay in relaying her concerns, she interrupted whatever he was trying to tell her. "What? Ben, I can't hear you. Where are you? Can you move to a room with better reception?"

"Not...room," he said, his voice louder but the reception only marginally clearer.

"Where are you?" she repeated.

"I'm...call...Prescott County."

"You're in Prescott County? Why?"

He unleashed a stream of distorted words and heavy breathing. She thought she heard him say the word "body" and might have made a joke about obscene phone calls if he didn't sound so serious. And urgent.

"Why are you huffing and puffing?"

"Trying...hang on...a clearing," he said, the connection clearing at last. "There. Better?"

"Much better. Did you have to climb a hill or something?"

"Or something." Ben inhaled deeply, then said in a rush, "They called me when we got off the phone earlier. They found a body."

Her breath snarled in her throat. Her mouth ran dry. All she could force out was a strangled, "Oh, God."

"We have an ID on the victim, but I can't tell you yet. We're looking into next of kin. Listen, I'm at the scene now, and things are hectic. I have to get back there, but I'm probably going to lose you. It's not terribly developed around here," he said, faltering a bit on the last.

"Most of Prescott County is pretty rural," she managed in a whisper.

"Yeah." His voice softened and he spoke quietly into the phone. "Marlee, can you come see me first thing in the morning?"

"I can stop by when I go for my run. Why? What

do you need?"

"They found the body in a half-finished house…on the other side of Sawtooth Lake."

Chapter Eleven

Marlee rolled out of bed, tied her hair up in a messy bun and put on her running shoes. The sun peeped over the horizon. She hadn't slept a wink. Between keeping a watchful eye on her window, replaying the run-in with Will Thomason in her head from every different angle and wondering who'd been found dead on the other side of Sawtooth Lake, she hadn't been able to put her mind on pause long enough to even doze.

Marlee stretched, then took off toward the municipal building at a brisk jog. She'd worked up to a pretty good clip by the time she reached the door to the sheriff's office with the flats of her palms. She looked up and saw Mike Schaeffer's pale, shocked face on the other side of the glass. He raised both hands in surprise, then took a step back so she could enter.

"Hey," she said, breathless. "I'm Marlee Masters. We weren't properly introduced the other day. You're Mike?" She raised her arms over her head in an effort to open her lungs and even out her breathing.

"Um, yes. Yes, ma'am," the deputy stammered.

Swallowing her annoyance, she thrust out a hand. "Not 'ma'am.' Marlee."

He gaped at her for a moment, then gave her hand a brief but firm shake. "Yes, ma—Marlee."

"Marlee?" Ben's deep voice startled Mike into dropping her hand.

"I was goin', but she came runnin' up," the younger man explained in a rush.

Ben nodded his understanding. "She has a way of sneaking up on people. Go on home, Mike. You did good work tonight." The younger man looked unsure, so Ben waved him on. "I'll be leaving here right behind you. Get some rest."

Once the outer door closed, he spoke to Marlee in a hushed rush. "I don't want to talk here."

"But I heard—"

He grasped her elbow and nudged her closer to the door. "I need to talk to you about some stuff, but this is not the time or the place."

She caught his urgency but couldn't follow his logic. They were in the sheriff's office. Another person was dead, and she assumed he might now be giving her suspicions of foul play more credence. What better time? What better place?

His dark eyes bore into her. "Fine," she managed at last. "Where? When?"

"What time do you have to be at the office?"

"I'm going to be working out of Wendell's office. He told me he prefers banker's hours, so not until nine o'clock."

He nodded. "Go run. Meet me at my place. I should

be able to shake free from here in about twenty minutes."

"Your place?"

"Yeah. It's a blue house with awnings down the street about—"

"The Larkins' place," she said, pinpointing the house he meant on her internal map.

He nodded. "His daughter rented it to me. He moved to a place in Florida to be closer to her."

She nodded but refused to be distracted by the details. She could get the scoop on the high school's long-time PE teacher later. "Your house. Twenty minutes," she agreed. "And be prepared to spill, because I'm not particularly good at waiting for what I want."

Without another glance, she backed out of the door and forced herself to break into a trot. She'd run for exactly nineteen minutes and forty-six seconds when she hooked a sharp left off the sidewalk and onto the brick walkway leading to the freshly painted front door of the house Ben Kinsella now called home.

More than once, she'd herded Jeff up these porch steps, a bulging trick-or-treat bag bumping against her leg. Mrs. Larkin made the world's most delicious popcorn balls every year. She felt a pang of sadness as she realized that even in Pine Bluff, people probably didn't hand out homemade treats anymore.

Ben opened the door the second her foot hit the top step. Sleep deprived and freaked out about what he might tell her, she had to blink twice at the man framed in the doorway. Unlike any of the Larkins, his head nearly touched the top of the door frame.

"Hey," he said, his voice creaking as he held the screen door open wide in invitation.

She stepped into the dimly lit entry and peered up at him. "Who was it?"

He shook his head, then gently closed the door behind her, cocooning them in the small space. "I think you'd better sit down."

"Who was it?"

"I'm told you were acquainted with the victim." He drew out his notebook but didn't bother opening it. "The victim's name was Beaufort Abernathy."

Marlee gasped, then pressed her lips together to ward off the hot prickle of tears clogging her throat. "Bo," she managed at last.

"Yes." He fidgeted with the still-unopened notebook. "I'm told the two of you used to date?"

She stared at him uncomprehendingly for a moment. "Date?"

This time, he flipped open the cover on the tiny pad, but his eyes never dropped to the page. "Yes."

"We, uh," she stammered, the fog of shock lifting. "Yeah. In high school. We, um, we went to prom." She scowled when she realized he wasn't taking any of this information down. As a matter of fact, he wasn't even holding a pen. "I take it you knew all this already," she ventured.

"Yes."

His succinct answer made goose bumps rise on her skin, but she refused to lead her own interrogation.

"His wife mentioned you."

"Wife?"

"Kayla Abernathy," he supplied.

She searched her memory. "I don't think I'm familiar with anyone named Kayla."

"She said she was behind you in school."

"Okay," Marlee responded, drawing the word out encouragingly.

"She also says it's your fault he's dead."

Marlee recoiled. "My fault?" She shook her head. "How—why would she…? Wait, Mrs. Brewster said something about a suicide. Did Bo Abernathy shoot himself?"

Ben nodded solemnly. "Single gunshot wound at close range. Weapon at the scene. No sign of a struggle or anything indicating anyone else was there." He hesitated. "Wait, no. I take that back. There was lots of evidence of other people being on the scene, but most of it could be attributed to the construction." A shadow of a smile ghosted across his lips, but it didn't have the oomph to reach his tired eyes. "Let's say the Prescott County deputies were, uh, enthusiastic when they reached the scene." He jerked his head toward the living room. "Come in. I need to sit, or I'll fall over."

Marlee followed him to the floral-print sofa she'd lay odds came with the house. "So, how could it be my fault?"

"Mrs. Abernathy claims the two of you were having an affair."

Her jaw actually dropped. "An affair?" she parroted.

He nodded, his expression somber. "She says he's been talking about you ever since you came back to town."

"Oh, my God," she breathed. "The texts? Do you think they were from Bo?"

"Can't say for certain until we can get a look at the computer and cell phone," he hedged.

"Damn. Bo Abernathy." She gave her head a rueful shake. "I've only spoken to him once since I've been back. It was at…"

She trailed off, and he leaned in. "It was at…" he prompted.

She pressed the tips of her fingers to her lips. "Clint's visitation."

Without prompting, she gave him a brief overview of her relationship with Bo in high school, the last time she'd seen him before she left for college and the hellos they'd exchanged at the funeral home.

Ben nodded, then closed the notebook again, apparently satisfied with her answer. "I'll need to take a statement from you regarding, uh, your whereabouts last night."

"My whereabouts?" she asked distractedly. "You know where I was. I was with you at the lake one night, and the next I drove my mother to a meeting."

He sighed heavily. "Yes, and now our trip to the lake will be part of the records. I'll ask Lori to take it so there's no conflict of interest." His expression grave, he met her eyes. "I'm sorry."

She straightened her shoulders. "Why are you sorry? I'm not ashamed to be with you, Ben."

"I know, but…" He shot her a baleful look. "I don't want to open you up to any gossip."

"Gossip?" She gave a short, bitter laugh. "You know

small towns guzzle gossip like gasoline. The talk about me started the day I was born and likely won't die until I do. It's nothing I can't handle."

"I know, but with everything else." He made a circling motion with his hand. "I'm sorry. I understand the text thing has been weighing on you, and hopefully we'll have some answers for that. And I have to tell you, I'm coming around to the way you are thinking about these deaths more and more, but I've been up all day and all night and I am beat."

She nodded. "I didn't sleep well either."

"Did it have something to do with why you called me?"

She started to tell him about her run-in with Will Thomason but stammered to a stop. "It'll keep."

He stared at her, his gaze intense. "Are you sure? I'm not trying to put you off." He held her hand, and she'd swear she felt her bones melt away. "I'm so damn tired."

"I understand."

"We need to talk," he said, lowering her hand with a squeeze and a wistful sigh. "We have to talk about ugly things, and I hate it. I don't want to talk to you about this stuff."

"What do you want to talk about?"

She couldn't help herself. One of them was going to have to give voice to this attraction between them, and she wanted him to speak first. She could no longer play it cool with this man. She wanted to discover exactly what he wanted from her. Then she wanted to find a way to give it to him.

When she looked into his eyes again, he looked so vulnerable, so raw, it scared her. "Anything other than death."

She nodded as they stood. "Get some rest. Maybe we can meet for lunch and fill each other in?"

"Great." His voice cracked with exhaustion.

Then the world caught fire.

He kissed her. Not an accidental brush or a friendly peck but a full-on kiss. His lips were soft but firm. He slid one big hand into her hair, tangling his fingers in the strands caught up in her ponytail and pulling hard enough to extract a soft moan. His other hand found her hip as she wrapped her arms around his waist, clutching at the hard ridges of muscle bracketing his spine. She angled her head, hoping for a better fit, but as quickly as it started, it stopped.

Ben released her so quickly, she stumbled back a step. She touched her fingertips to her tingling lips.

"I'm sorry."

His apology came out rough and ragged. The heat in his eyes told her he was lying. He wasn't sorry. Neither was she. But she couldn't resist baiting him to see if she could make him own it.

"Are you?"

"I shouldn't have."

Her heart fluttered in protest, but she kept her voice steady. "No?"

"No."

"Why not?"

"Because I—" He broke off, running his palm over

his hair. She was the one who'd been mussed, but he kept smoothing those close-cropped curls.

She ached to knock his hand away and smooth them herself. Instead, she took her fingers from her lips and pressed them to his mouth. "I wanted you to kiss me."

"I know, but—"

He spoke the protest against her fingers. She laughed and lowered her hand. "Stop with the buts," she ordered. "As a matter of fact, as an attorney, I would advise you to stop speaking altogether. You're sleep-deprived. Crazy, horrible things are happening all around us. But there's nothing you can say to erase that kiss."

"I don't want to erase—"

She pressed her fingertips to his lips again. When his shoulders sagged in capitulation, she pulled her hand down to uncover those warm, delicious lips and cradled his chin in her hand as she rose up to kiss him again. He sighed against her mouth, then gathered her snug against him once more.

This time, she broke the kiss, tipping her head down until she felt his fast, shallow breaths stirring her hair. She sighed happily when he pressed a tender kiss to the top of her head.

"Get some sleep," she said, grasping his strong arms as she pried herself away. "I have to get home and get ready for work."

MARLEE PULLED THE cardigan she'd carried with her into the Wingate Law Firm close around her as she stared down at the open folder in front of her. She'd shivered the previous day away in her silk blouse and pencil skirt. She'd felt much better about today's outfit. The skirt was fuller and longer than its predecessor. Cut in an A-line silhouette, it was at once flattering but more concealing. She'd paired it with a lightweight summer sweater and matching cardigan. Each time the vent above the table whirred to life, she congratulated herself on her forethought.

Dora, Wendell's longtime secretary, poked her head around the door and flaunted her mind-reading skills. "He leaves for court over in Prescott County in ten minutes," she said in a hush. "I gave the thermostat a bump. Hang in there."

Marlee beamed her gratitude. "You're a saint."

Dora rolled her eyes. "I've been freezing my what-sis off for nearly thirty years," she said dryly. "I have a space heater under my desk and a blanket in the bottom file cabinet if you start seeing icicles hanging off the end of your nose."

"I'm good for now. Thank you."

The moment the older woman pulled the door closed, Marlee refocused on the fat file in front of her. To anyone not used to digging through miles of legalese, the work would have seemed tedious, but she found it fascinating.

The endless stream of documents exchanged between attorneys representing two or more parties were nothing more than the movement of legal chess pieces. A proposal, an answer. Counterproposals, demands, refusal, injunctions and subpoenas. These were all small moves made in the course of a larger game. Each party had an objective in mind. Legal wrangling boiled down to what was essentially a footrace run with words.

Her father had been receiving offers for property on Sawtooth Lake for decades. Developer after developer came to him with ever-growing pots of money. Over the years, he'd also fended off the end-around moves made by people hoping to claim that land owned by the Masters family actually belonged to the great state of Georgia. Henry had come out on top each time, thanks in large part to Wendell Wingate's seemingly limitless patience.

Wendell never thrust when he could parry. He raised sidestepping to an art form and wielded a deft hand at drafting motions designed to set his opponents scrambling. The more she read through the files, the greater her respect for her new mentor. She didn't doubt he'd make a fair-minded and highly influential judge.

"How is it coming?"

Wendell stood in the doorway, watching her. "Good," she said automatically. "I'm fine." To her surprise, she realized she was telling the truth. She was fine. Tired and worried, but the work helped. The work made sense. "Off to court?"

"I am." The older man straightened. "This is my last court appearance."

"On this side of the bench," she corrected.

"Precisely. The power of positive thinking."

"When is Simon coming to town?"

"In about a month." Wendell shifted his briefcase from one hand to the other, clearly anxious to be off. "Gives me time to wrap up some other routine matters I have in progress and get you up to speed on your family's pending business. Once he gets here, I'll start campaigning in earnest."

"If you don't mind, I may need you to come with me to the sheriff's office this afternoon. They want a statement regarding where I was last night in conjunction with Bo Abernathy's death."

"A statement? From you?" Wendell's forehead puckered. "I thought they were saying it was self-inflicted."

"They are, but apparently his wife thinks we were carrying on where we left off in high school."

His bushy white eyebrows rose. "Were you?"

"I was with Ben Kinsella at the lake one night. My father was home when he dropped me off," she stated flatly. "I drove my mother to a committee meeting the next night. Plenty of witnesses there."

He digested her recitation, then nodded. "Should be a quick statement, then." He checked his watch. "Okay. I'll meet you here after court. Now, I must go, or I'll be late for my last day."

Marlee stared at the door long after he departed. She'd never thought about Wendell campaigning for his seat on the bench. She'd assumed with her father backing him, the seat as their district's superior court bench would be Wendell's for the taking. She'd forgotten it wasn't an appointment but an elected position. No matter who was backing him, Wendell had to put his name on a ballot and hope people voted for him.

Thanking her lucky stars she had no such ambitions, she pulled the next file in the stack she'd collected to her and flipped open the cover, trying not to think about Bo Abernathy and the text messages she suspected he'd sent. Part of her was glad Wendell hadn't scanned and digitalized most of his old files. Staring at a computer for hours wasn't her idea of fun. Plus, seeing the facts laid out on paper sometimes made things she may have overlooked jump out at her.

Like the names neatly typed at the bottom of a document setting up a partnership agreement. It was for a consulting firm called White, Pinkman, Schrader and McGill. She snorted, then goggled at it, picking each letter out over and over until there was no question in her mind she was reading them correctly.

The names were too distinctive to be a coincidence. But only one person was likely to understand the subtle reference to a television show. Grabbing her phone, she tapped out a quick text to Ben.

Meet me at the Daisy for lunch when you get up. I have something wild to run past you.

Chapter Twelve

Ben stood outside the Daisy Drive-In, pacing back and forth under the short metal awning shading the old dairy bar's order and pick-up windows. It was high noon, and nearly all the now speakerless stalls were filled with people grabbing a quick bite in the air-conditioned comfort of their cars. Every now and then, one of the workers bustling behind the counter would slide open the glass on the pick-up window, shout a name or number through the screen or simply wave and point at a particular car. He'd visited less than a handful of times, but the veteran staff had his favorite menu items pegged. He chose to attribute this phenomenon to their skill. It felt homier than knowing the markings on his truck, the uniform he wore and his *newness* gave him away every time.

"Ben."

He stopped pacing and pivoted on his heel, stalking off in the direction of her voice, desperate to get to her as soon as possible. His gut was telling him Marlee was right when she labeled what was happening around them murder rather than suicide. If she had an inkling as to what tied them together, the knowledge might place her in danger.

"Hey," he said, careful not to reach for her as he stopped on the sidewalk in front of her. "Tenders, sandwich or salad?" He scanned the letter-board menu posted high in the center window. "If you want the chicken-fried chicken, you have to come back on Wednesday. Today the special is catfish."

She elbowed him in the ribs. Darlene, one of the Daisy's longtime staff, watched the byplay between them with an amused smirk.

"Hey, Miss Darlene," Marlee cooed, stooping to peer closer at the woman. "How are you? How's your mama?"

"I'm fine and Mama's ornery as ever." Darlene leaned into the screen, her pencil and order pad at the ready. "Cheeseburger and pineapple shake?"

"Yes, ma'am. And throw in some onion rings," Marlee said cheerfully. "I need to feed the sheriff, stat. We've sure been keeping this poor man busy around here, haven't we?" She gave a pitying shake of her head.

Darlene hummed, then tsked softly. "I promise you, things are usually much quieter around here, Sheriff Ben. These past few years…" She shook her head, a mystified expression on her worry-lined face. "You want a club sandwich and sweet tea, or are you branchin' out today?" She craned her neck to peer up at him through the tiny square screen.

"I'll take a cheeseburger too," he said decisively, peeved to realize he'd fallen into patterns so easily followed. "And sweet tea."

"I'll holler for ya," Darlene promised, then slid the window shut with a thud loud enough to jolt him from his self-chastisement.

Ben shifted, uncomfortable despite the ease between the two women. He never used to be the kind of guy who had a regular order. He'd gotten soft. Or maybe he hadn't cared who followed him out here. Not at first. But now. He'd been careless. Forgetting for whole days he was a man with a target on his back, which was dangerous. Even all the way out here, in backwoods Georgia. He needed to be smarter. For his own sake, and for everyone around him.

"Let's go sit on the wall," Marlee said, tugging on his arm.

He glanced over at the woman beside him and his breath caught. She was the prototypical all-American girl. Her blond hair tumbled in loose waves over her shoulders, pulled back from her face by a narrow band of red elastic. She wore makeup, he was sure, but it didn't obscure the dusting of freckles on the bridge of her nose. The skirt she had on was full and fluffy, falling to her knees in swirling folds. It matched her headband, and the sweater. The sweater she wore was simple but fit snug over her slender figure. She had another long-sleeved sweater looped around her neck. Who wore sweaters tied around their neck in real life?

A strobe burst of memory slowed his steps as she led the way to the cinder block retaining wall encircling the property. White teeth and gold jewelry. His best friend standing in front of the city's biggest thug, holding an assault rifle. Willing to put his body between a stampede of federal agents and a weaselly white guy who wore a tennis sweater around his shoulders.

He could still see Andre's confusion melting away as he realized Ben was the only one who could have given them up to the authorities. But it all went to hell too fast. A blast of automatic-weapon fire on both sides. His weapon in his hand. Andre dropping to his knees, then pitching forward, the light gone from his eyes. They never told him if any of the bullets pulled out of his best friend's body actually came from his weapon, and he never asked.

In the end, all that mattered was Ivan Jones knew his name and his face, and his life in Atlanta was over. Forever.

"Ben?" Marlee called to him.

Shaking off the memory, he picked up the pace again. A smattering of people sat atop the wall in patches of shade provided by nearby trees planted on the neighboring property. He checked their faces. They were vaguely familiar, but there were relatively few people he knew on sight.

They picked a spot a good distance away from a pair of teenagers splitting an order of tater tots smothered in chili and cheese. He automatically reached for Marlee's arm to steady her as she hopped up to sit on the wall.

"Nice sweater," he said, nodding to the cardigan looped around her shoulders.

"Thanks. I had to dress in layers. Wendell keeps the thermostat set at meat locker."

His attention drifted to her bare calves as she crossed her ankles. She wore shiny red high heels.

The shoes would definitely have drawn the attention of her secret admirer. If he'd lived to see them.

"Have you received more texts?" He sounded edgy, even to his own ears, but he cut himself some slack. He was running on less than five hours' sleep in the past forty-eight.

"No." She patted the wall beside her. "Sit." She shifted to face him more fully. "I have to tell you something."

"Okay," he replied warily.

"I called you last night to tell you I had a run-in with my dad's minion, Will Thomason, and until this morning, he was number one on my possible creeper list."

"What? Why?" He scowled, pushing down the urge to plant a fist in the guy's face merely on her say-so. "What do you mean, 'run-in'?"

Without a clue about his inner turmoil, Marlee proceeded to tell him about the mystery involving her drapes and how she'd been traipsing around her house in nothing but a towel the previous night.

Ben's hands curled into fists. He looked everywhere but at her, needing a moment to get a handle on the rage roiling inside him. Marlee would neither welcome nor appreciate any kind of caveman reaction, so he needed to keep the lid clamped down tight.

"Long story, and we'll get to it, but let me tell you what I found this morning."

Ben wanted to bow up at being put off, but she was so obviously bursting to share, he didn't have the heart to disappoint her. "What do you want to tell me?"

"I was going through all these papers, trying to draw

some more lines between the members of the Sportsmen's Club and my brother, and I came across a consulting firm with a funny name."

He narrowed his eyes. "Funny how?"

"They set themselves up not long after the furor from the DEA operation died down. They call themselves White, Pinkman, Schrader and McGill."

He shook his head, momentarily confused. "Is this the wild thing you mentioned?" She nodded, and then something clicked. "What were the names again?" He gaped at her as she patiently repeated them.

"White, Pinkman, Schrader and McGill."

"Like the characters from *Breaking Bad*?"

She nodded, pleasure lighting her face. "I knew you'd get it. I imagine a lot of you DEA guys watched that show."

He shrugged. "Some did. It was good television, but to be honest with you, most of us were annoyed they made a sort-of hero out of Walter White."

"Yes, well, I found an offer to buy the land at Sawtooth Lake from this group." She shrugged. "Not the first, but it was the one my brother took to my father."

"And Henry rejected it."

She confirmed his assumption with a brief nod. "Then later reached out to them to accept it. But by then, another party was involved. A real estate investment group represented by Jared Baker. The guy I wanted to go work for in Atlanta."

This was the first he'd heard of any plans Marlee had extending beyond Pine Bluff. Of course it would be Atlanta. The one place in the world he'd never step foot in again. Not even on a layover, if he could help it. "You planned to remain in Atlanta," he said, keeping his voice as even as he could.

She waved a fluttering hand as if her plans were inconsequential. "Yeah, well, the best-laid plans of Masters children and all," she said dismissively.

She was speaking in riddles, and he didn't have the patience to unravel them now. "What kind of law was it?"

"Corporate but medium-sized. Not the flashy stuff." She shrugged. "Doesn't matter. My father made sure I couldn't get an interview, much less the job. This morning I saw Baker's name on the papers."

Ben took a moment to digest the information. "Jared Baker is connected to the Sawtooth Lake Sportsmen's Club, this partnership, and you were supposed to interview for a job with him?"

"Sheriff Ben!" Darlene shouted from the window of the dairy bar.

Marlee nodded and picked up her phone as he slid down from the wall. "You grab the food, and I'll pull up their website and text it to you."

Ben's mind raced, parsing the sentence for pertinent information then filing bits away to be reviewed later. Marlee planned to leave Pine Bluff. That knowledge had to be stowed away for now too. He had to focus on what was happening around Sawtooth Lake. He heard the chime of a text alert as he reached for his wallet to pay for their lunch. "What do I owe you?"

Darlene waved him off. "Nothing. I charged it to Henry's account."

He stared at her, dumbfounded. "You run tabs for people?"

Smirking, she said, "I run a tab for Henry Masters." Then she slid the window shut with a metallic thwack, indicating the end of the conversation.

Clutching their food and drinks, he hurried back to the spot where Marlee sat waiting for him. Upon approach, he wagged his head in exaggerated dismay. "This town is nuttier than a fruitcake."

She beamed as she extracted her milkshake from his hands. "You're only noticing it now?"

He placed the bag between them, then resumed his seat on the wall. "I guess I'm getting used to seeing more instances of nuttiness hanging out with you."

She smiled, then dug into the bag and removed two foil-wrapped burgers along with a paper boat filled with onion rings.

He studied her closely. "You seem to be bearing up well," he observed mildly.

She lowered her sunglasses to peer at him over the frames. "So far, I've lost my brother and two men I've known most of my life." She pushed the glasses up and took a bite of an onion ring, chewing while she let the information sink in. "I can't think too hard about it now."

"Marlee, I—"

"Can we take ten minutes?" Her eyes implored him. "I found the information, and I will talk about it. But I didn't stop to think what it might mean beyond sort of filling in the blanks. And I want—" She broke off. Her gaze dropped to the remaining bite pinched between her fingers. "I want us to eat lunch together like normal people. Maybe talk about something other than death while we do it?" She grimaced. "Do I sound horrible?"

He looked into her big blue eyes, and something inside him uncoiled. "No. I get you," he answered quietly. "Ten minutes isn't going to hurt anyone." He set to work unwrapping his cheeseburger. "I haven't tried a burger yet."

She stared at him, shock widening her eyes as she chewed. "You haven't?"

"There are too many other things. Even I can cook a burger," he said with a shrug.

She snorted and set to work unwrapping her own sandwich. "Not a Daisy burger," she asserted. "You'd better try an onion ring too. They're life changing."

Ben eyed the thick burger. "They are, huh?"

She reached for another of the lightly battered rings and held it so close to his eyes, he could pick out the flecks of pepper in the breading. "You'll swear you saw God this day, Ben Kinsella. Mark my words," she intoned gravely.

Chuckling, he took the onion ring from her and let it dangle from his index finger as he took a big bite of the burger. Juicy, well-seasoned beef made his taste buds sing. He closed his eyes for a moment, then widened them at her as he chewed, letting out an appreciative moan.

Beside him, Marlee laughed and wriggled, delighted by the small triumph. "Told you so. The ring is going to blow your mind."

THEY ATE QUICKLY but kept the conversation mercifully light. Selfishly, she wanted to sit with Ben in the dappled sunlight, eating cheeseburgers and talking about their favorite fried foods. She needed a moment of normalcy, even if it was a bit forced. People cast curious glances in their direction, but she didn't care. She was happy sharing a slice of peace with him.

They split the last onion ring between them. She watched as Ben sucked a bit of burger grease from his finger and thumb, then handed over the remaining, yet wholly inadequate, paper napkin. He took his time wiping his hands. "You ready to talk more now?"

Marlee sighed, a blush warming her cheeks as she balled up her own napkin and tossed it into the paper bag. "Yeah, I guess."

"You're the one who came to me with your suspicions," he reminded her gently. "We aren't the ones making these things happen. If they are connected, if there is something going on, don't you think we owe it to your brother to figure out what it is?"

"Yes."

"We're going to need to have a handle on everything you can unearth about this property deal."

She nodded. "Right. But I think you'd better make it more official. Come to Wendell's office this afternoon. We'll tell him what we suspect and let him decide what he wants to tell my father and when."

The corner of his mouth lifted. "You want me to give your father the chance to lawyer up?"

"My father doesn't need to be any more lawyered up than he already is. Besides, he has as much of an interest in seeing this solved as I do. More, even. He's the one who has had to live with my mother day in and day out since Jeff died," she added quietly. "Maybe it will help him to realize she hasn't been entirely off the mark."

He nodded, then dropped down off the wall. She scrambled to gather her wits and her belongings, but he snatched up their trash in one hand and offered her the other. Grasping her discarded cardigan, she placed her fingertips in his palm and allowed him to steady her as she gained her footing. To her surprise, he closed his fingers around hers, hanging tight to her hand as they made their way toward the trash bins. They'd almost made it past the front bumper of Reverend Mitchell's Buick when he remembered himself.

He tried to drop her hand, but Marlee was having none of his nonsense. She made a show of sliding on the loose gravel at the edge of the pavement and hooked her wrist through his arm. When she flipped her hair back over her shoulder, she tossed a friendly wave toward her family's minister.

"Afternoon, Reverend Mitchell," she called, squeezing Ben's bicep to halt him.

He shot her a glare but obliged as the clergyman rolled his window down.

"Good afternoon," the older man called to them. "It's nice to see you home, Miss Marlee."

"Good to be home," she lied through bared teeth. "I assume you've met Sheriff Kinsella," she added.

"Yes, we have met," the minister said genially. "Sheriff, I hope you're settling in? We'd love to see you some Sunday."

Ben stiffened slightly under her grasp, but he gave the older man a respectful nod. "Kind of you, Reverend. I appreciate the invitation."

"I have to get on back to work," Marlee said, using the hand holding her sweater to wave. "You say hello to Mrs. Mitchell for me."

"You can tell her hello yourself on Sunday," the minister replied. "See you, Miss Marlee." Without waiting for her reply, he grinned and rolled his window up again.

Marlee laughed, hugging Ben's arm to her side as he led the way. "Darn, I walked smack into that trap, didn't I?"

She beamed up at him, but the moment was shattered when her phone dinged to indicate a new text message. A creeping sensation crawled up her spine as she pulled her phone out. Forcing a smile to trigger the device's facial recognition, she stopped dead when she saw the message notification from an unknown number.

No one wants you here, Marlee. Go away!

BEN RESENTED HAVING to return to the sheriff's office. Every minute he spent parted from Marlee made him itchy. Aside from the text that blew his theory out of the water, he wanted to be with her when she shared the information she'd unearthed about the land sale with Wingate so he could gauge the man's reaction. Right now, only the two of them knew about the land, and he wanted to keep it that way for now. What was the old saying? Two people can keep a secret, but three people can only keep one if two of them are dead.

Whether Marlee was aware of it or not, there was inherent risk in sharing her findings with Wendell Wingate. They had no clue who could be mixed up in whatever this was, but Wendell Wingate was aware of the land transactions. If he hadn't already been asking himself questions about the circumstances between Jeff Masters's death and Clint Young's, adding Bo Abernathy's to the mix should certainly set the gears to grinding.

They'd have to watch Wingate carefully. The attorney was too sharp, too skilled a lawyer to have any of the obvious tells. This was where his status as someone new to the area could help. His impressions of Wingate would be fresh and unfiltered.

Sitting at his desk, he scrolled through the Baker Law Firm website, scouring every page for a clue connecting the man to Masters County and Sawtooth Lake. But he found none. The guy was an Atlanta native. Buckhead area, of course. He'd attended Pace Academy, gone north to Harvard for undergrad and law school and then come back to practice. He'd spent only two years as an associate at one of the city's prestigious firms prior to striking out on his own.

From what he could find, the firm's client base was

more eclectic than the corporations they represented at his old firm. There were a couple of deep-pocket corporations, of course, but also a mix of financial wizards, athletes, a reality television star and some hotshots from the local rap scene on their client roster. He lingered over an article linking Jared Baker to a gang-connected rapper whose name Ben recognized from the time he spent embedded in the SEATL crew. He closed out of the screen with a growl of frustration.

Spinning away from the computer, he tapped his forefinger to his upper lip as he weighed the possibilities. Also, divulging their suspicions might cause any of the people involved to go to ground—which would be good and bad. Good because it might bring a halt to these horrific scenes but bad because the how or why behind it would remain a mystery.

He sighed and pushed out of his desk chair. He'd stalled as long as he could. He needed to get over to Wingate's offices and start fitting puzzle pieces together. He also needed to talk to Marlee about keeping her nose out of the investigation. There was a time and place for attorneys, but usually, it came later.

Now, he needed to be a cop.

As much as he hated to admit it given the circumstances, for the first time in a long time, it felt good again.

Chapter Thirteen

Wendell sat in his desk chair, his elbows propped on the arms and his fingers steepled beneath his chin, his attention fixed on Ben. Marlee fought the urge to interject facts here and there while Ben methodically laid out the details surrounding the deaths of Jeff Masters, Clint Young and now Bo Abernathy, as well as the connection Marlee had drawn between the three men and the sale of her family's property at Sawtooth Lake. Any information she had in addition to the facts Ben so painstakingly outlined would have been an exercise in gilding the lily. All they had at the moment were three deaths without any evidence pointing to anything beyond suicide and a basket full of supposition, so she kept her mouth shut and let Wendell's sharply honed intellect do the work.

When Ben finished speaking, the older man ran the tips of his interlaced fingers back and forth under his chin. The moment lasted an eternity. He puffed out his cheeks and exhaled a long, weary breath. "Well," he said, his voice creaking from disuse. He cleared his throat and gripped the arm of his chair, sitting straighter. "I don't have to point out your complete lack of evidence," he said meaningfully.

"No, sir," Ben and Marlee said in unrehearsed unison.

They shared a glance, then Ben quickly pinned his attention on the man across the desk. "But you have to admit, there's something off with all this."

Wendell nodded thoughtfully as he stared at Ben, apparently taking the sheriff's measure in a new light. "Here I thought you'd come to Pine Bluff to get away from all this sort of ugliness."

The older man's words were light, but she picked up the mocking edge. Marlee slid forward in her leather club chair and leaned in, ready to put herself between the two men if necessary. But it wasn't necessary. Ben was more than capable of handling himself.

"Masters County has always had its fair share of ugliness, Mr. Wingate." His voice was deep and steady, carrying a clipped note of command. He wasn't easily bullied. "You know it and I knew it when I took the job."

"So you did," Wendell conceded with a nod. Yanking his hands apart, he let his arms fall open, palmsup, in an indication of futility. "You have no evidence."

"Not a bit," Ben confirmed, not backing down.

"What do you propose to do?"

Ben glanced over at Marlee, and she jumped, startled to realize she'd nearly missed her cue. "Uh…" Looking at Ben, she forged ahead. "I saw the parcel where the house was being built was owned by an

Abernathy. I assumed it belonged to Bill and Allison Abernathy."

To her surprise, Wendell shook his head. "No, it was young Bo who bought it."

Marlee reared back, shocked by the revelation.

"Bo?" she asked, incredulous. His bushy white brows rose, and she caught the movement of Ben's head out of the corner of her eye, but she couldn't tear her gaze from Wendell. Not until he confirmed they were speaking of the same person.

"Yes, Bo Abernathy. I believe the two of you were an item once, weren't you?"

"Yes. I mean—" She huffed, frustrated with her inability to get her thoughts straight, much less her words. "We dated in high school, is all," she said dismissively. She pushed her point with Wendell. "I saw the sale prices on those parcels. I thought maybe his parents had sold their place in town to move out there or something. Where would Bo get so much money?"

The attorney blinked twice. "I did not handle the closing on each property. They took care of transfer at the Farmers Bank and Trust, but I assume he procured a loan."

She shook her head in disbelief. "But...he's my age. How could he raise the down payment in such a short time? Where does he work?"

This time Wendell didn't bother to hide his amusement. "Bo went to work for Georgia Mutual Insurance after he finished school, I believe. They put him through their training program, and he took over Gary Behrend's agency when he retired. Did you expect he'd dry up into a husk once you left town, Miss Marlee?"

She opened and shut her mouth, outraged by the shot at her ego. It hit too close to home.

"I met this guy," Ben said, breaking the tension of the moment. "Tried to sell me life insurance in the middle of the Piggly Wiggly the first week I moved here."

"Sounds about right," Wendell drawled. "That's where the money is." He paused, then chuckled. "In life insurance, I mean. Not the Piggly Wiggly."

"He bought into this land deal," Marlee interrupted. "Who's the head of this Sportsmen's Club anyway? Do they have a president or something?"

"Yes, they have a nominal president who acts as mediator in any disputes," Wendell said and then pursed his lips enough to give Marlee the impression he didn't approve of the person holding this position or maybe how they were doing their job.

"I suppose it's my father," she said, eyeing him warily.

Wingate shook his head. "No. It isn't. Originally, it was your brother, but after he…passed, Will Thomason took over the job. I suspect he thought it would be too much for your father, given the circumstances and all."

"Will Thomason," Marlee breathed, recoiling in her chair even as she spoke his name.

Wendell maintained his poker face. "Why? Is there an issue with Will?"

"I suspect Bo Abernathy had been sending me creepy text messages since I came back to town," she informed him. If the sudden change of subject threw the older man, he didn't show it. "The texter was using some kind of computer program to send messages from random numbers. His wife must have discovered the plot and immediately jumped to the conclusion we were sleeping together."

"Of course," Wendell said, barely batting an eyelash.

"But up until today, I thought it might have been Will Thomason." She grimaced, shooting Ben a smirk. "We didn't exactly hit it off."

This time, Wendell did raise his bushy eyebrows. "How odd. Most people seem to like Will."

"Yeah, well, I'm not most people." Eager to bypass any possibility of having to tell the towel story again, she plowed ahead. "Apparently, he and my father were doing some work into the evening."

Mr. Wingate steepled his fingers under his chin again. "Not unusual."

Marlee darted a look at Ben. "He was a bit over-familiar," she said, choosing her words carefully.

"How so?" Ben's voice was a growl.

She shook her head. "Nothing overt. We'd never met, but his comments were fairly laced with innu-endo." She met Wendell's eyes because she didn't dare let Ben get a good read on how much Thomason's behavior truly bothered her. "It was disconcerting."

"But you have met him," Wendell insisted, clearly puzzled.

She shook her head. "Not that I recall."

Wendell pursed his lips, then expelled a tired sigh. "Well, it's possible you were never properly introduced, but he was at Jeff's services. He was at your house after we came back from the cemetery. I recall speaking to him while we were in line to fill our plates."

Marlee cast her thoughts back to those horribly muzzy days surrounding her brother's death and interment, but no matter how hard she tried, she could not conjure the vaguest memory of ever having seen Will Thomason. Shaking her head, she said, "If he was there, we were never introduced. He's a good-looking man. I think I would have remembered."

Beside her, Ben made an inarticulate grunt, and she looked over, her lips curving. "What? It was only an observation."

"If you like the type."

She snickered. "Sheriff, I assure you there aren't many women over thirteen or under ninety who'd disagree. The man is empirically handsome. Doesn't make him attractive."

"You said he was, uh, forward with you last night," Wendell interrupted, yanking them back to the crux of the subject.

"Not forward," Marlee said, considering her words carefully. "More along the lines of sly and presumptive."

"This led you to *presume* he is the one sending you these anonymous messages," he said, tossing her word back at her.

"I thought he might be the one sending them," she admitted. "But now we have reason to believe it was another member of the Sawtooth Lake Sportsmen's Club. We came here because we want to get more information on the sale of the lake property."

The lawyer pounced. "You think they may be connected?"

"I think it's an odd coincidence we've had three apparent suicides in the area in the last year and they have all happened in cabins on Sawtooth Lake," Ben interjected smoothly.

"And all members of this Sportsmen's Club," she added.

"Three suicides," Wendell corrected. "Rulings were made on two of those deaths, and by your own account, we have no reason to suspect anything different will come from the coroner's office on poor Bo." He folded his hands atop his desk and peered at them over the top of his reading glasses. "If you would allow me to play devil's advocate for a moment?"

Ben inclined his head. "You probably won't say anything we're not already thinking, but go ahead."

"Well, I don't want to be a bore," Wendell drawled. "I can tell you if whoever you wanted to accuse came to me for a defense, I would snap the case up in a heartbeat. Big win, easy money and some sensational press to boot." He leaned forward, his expression earnest. "I understand you want a reason for what happened with Jeff, darlin'. We all do. Unfortunately, there's nothing there to justify a formal inquiry."

Marlee persisted. "What's the scoop on the Sportsmen's Club? How did it come to be?"

Wingate sighed as he sank back in his chair. "It's as I told you. Your brother was overseeing the real estate portion of the family business. Things were pretty rough in all the fallout from the DEA operation." At this, he shot a meaningful look at Ben, who simply met the other man's stare, unflinching and unapologetic. "The Masters land trust needed an infusion of cash, and your father refused to liquidate any of the company's direct holdings."

"Of course. He'd bankrupt himself before jeopardizing the business itself," Marlee said with a hint of acid in her tone.

"Rightly so." Wendell sat up again. "He could use the business to rebuild the family's fortune, but it would be nearly impossible to rebuild the business in this day and age. As it is, he's beating the corporate competition off with a flimsy stick. If word got out we were willing to sell even one inch of Timber Masters acreage, the big boys would have been on him like fire ants."

"They want to buy him out," she concluded.

"When everything went down with the methamphetamine labs, the company was vulnerable for a number of reasons." He rubbed his chin thoughtfully. "Your daddy wondered if maybe some of those operations might have had some form of 'corporate' sponsorship."

His openly questioning gaze landed on Ben. "Do they do that?"

Ben shook his head. "Yes and no. You likely wouldn't have been able to make a direct connection. Most of the profits flowed into or through Atlanta. Most of it was scrubbed. Laundered. It's a chicken-and-egg sort of business model."

"So his suspicions would not have been completely out of left field?" Wendell pressed.

"No more so than Marlee's belief these three deaths may have something more than means and location in common. We need to figure out what the motivation might have been."

Rather than conceding the point, Wendell closed his eyes, drew in a deep breath and held it. He released it with a long hiss. Marlee would swear she could see the man deflating, though he didn't alter his posture one bit. "Motivation is never the difficult part. Most crimes boil down to a handful of motivating factors. Money is probably number one, followed by the misplaced pride we call love," he said with a cynical laugh. "Hell, you can find a list of them in the Bible." He pinned her with a shrewd gaze. "And don't bother arguing gluttony only leads to self-inflicted wounds. I can tell you about the day Betsy Lovell shot her husband of thirty-two years because the man had the gall to eat the last Little Debbie in the box."

Undeterred by the older man's dissertation on the seven deadly sins, Marlee steered the conversation back on course. "The land was purchased by a trust set up in the names of White, Pinkman, Schrader and McGill."

Wendell nodded. "Yes, but I do not believe the attorneys themselves were aware who was funding the trust. I spoke to Jared Baker on the phone, and he said he was excited to be purchasing his lot. Apparently, a friend of his grew up over in Prescott County and he wanted a place for long weekends, or to loan out to special clients during hunting seasons."

He swiveled his chair as he spoke, and the motion seemed to keep the words flowing.

"The land itself has some conservation provisions your grandfather had put in place. Dwellings could be built along the shoreline but only single-family homes. The sale of parcels had to be approved by the Timber Masters board. No commercial development. And there's a whole host of voluntary conservation provisions subject to oversight by the Environmental Protection Agency."

A burst of laughter escaped Marlee so suddenly, Ben jumped in his seat. His head swiveled and she held up a hand in apology. "Sorry," she said, then gasped through the fingers clamped over her mouth.

Wendell chuckled. Finally, he condescended to let Ben in on the joke. "Let's say the timber industry and the EPA have never been bosom buddies. It's been particularly contentious in the past ten years or so." He turned to Marlee. "But your grandpa was a clever one. He tried to hammer out a working relationship with them. Timber Masters survived when so many other companies of comparable size were so twisted up by regulations, they had no choice but to surrender to the conglomerates."

"Whoever bought the land had to agree to work within all these provisions," Ben clarified.

"Exactly. When they came up with the proposal for the Sportsmen's Club, it seemed the perfect solution. The land was already approved for hunting and fishing by the Department of Natural Resources, so as long as the members stayed within the guidelines, it was a natural fit, if you'll pardon the pun."

Marlee sobered as the pieces fell into place for her.

"So, after Jeff died, my father agreed to the plan, and Will Thomason took Jeff's place as president."

Since there was no evidence to suggest foul play found at any of the scenes at Sawtooth Lake, Ben couldn't make official inquiries. If anyone was going to talk to Will Thomason about the members of the Sportsmen's Club, it would have to be her. Except she wasn't looking forward to the task. With her lips thinned into a line, she pushed up from her chair. "Thanks for the background. We'll let you get back to your work."

Ben shot to his feet as well. "Thanks for your time." He practically chased Marlee from the room.

To HER RELIEF, Wendell didn't attempt to prolong the conversation, and Ben didn't feel the need to say anything more until after they'd left the attorney's inner sanctum and returned to the conference room where she'd been working. The moment she closed the door behind her, though, he shifted into full-on bossy alpha male.

"I don't want you trying to talk to any of these guys."

He was so authoritative, she might have obeyed if she weren't prepared for exactly this sort of order. "I will be talking to them," she replied calmly. "And I'll remind you that you have absolutely no business doing so yourself."

"How can you say I have no business?" he demanded hotly. "I'm the sheriff in this county."

"And as our chief law enforcement officer, you are

aware you don't have one sliver of probable cause to ask anyone anything related to these unfortunate and untimely deaths," she said, enunciating the last so pointedly, she was surprised the man didn't start to ooze blood.

"Marlee—"

"I, on the other hand, as the bereaved sister of one of the victims, am free to ask anyone anything I want," she stated officiously.

"These could be dangerous people," he argued. "Hell, you think one of them is keeping tabs on your bedroom window. If you think I'm gonna let you—"

"You don't '*let*' me do anything, Sheriff Kinsella," she said, cutting him off at the knees.

"Damn it, Marlee, you can't drag me into this thing then go off like some small-town Olivia Pope, all badass and ready to 'handle' things," he countered.

She blinked, surprised by the reference to the television show *Scandal* but not displeased by the comparison. "Olivia Pope. Good one. Who doesn't want to be a gladiator in a suit?"

"Stop," he growled.

"You started it," she said, jabbing him in the chest with her index finger.

He grabbed her finger, the heat of his skin sending tingles up her arm, then took hold of her entire hand. When she looked up into his eyes, she found them dark with worry and frustration.

"You can't do anything," she reminded him. "Not in an official capacity. And unofficially, no one is going to talk to you, Ben." She gentled the assertion with a wan smile. "They don't know you."

She winced, seeing the moment the simple truth of her statement hit home with him. He was an outsider and always would be. No matter how welcome they said he was. With a rumbling growl of frustration, he yanked on her hand, pulling her up against the solid wall of his chest.

"Do you always have to be right?"

She raised a shoulder. "I can't help it."

"And I can't help this."

He pressed his mouth to hers, crushing her lips beneath his. She welcomed the punishing force for the thrill it shot through her. When he softened the caress, his lips still clung to hers as he pulled back. They stared at one another, breathless and wanting but all too aware of their surroundings.

"Not sorry," he told her.

"Me either," she answered, lifting her free hand to caress his cheek.

"We're riding on the razor's edge here."

"Yes, we are."

"Marlee, I don't want you anywhere near Will Thomason without me around." He exhaled harshly. "I'm not trying to go all caveman on you. I… I'd be tearing my hair out the whole time."

She slid her hand up to massage his nape. "And it's such nice hair."

"Please," he said, his voice cracking.

She wasn't exactly sure what he was asking her for, but it didn't matter. Marlee was fairly certain they were on the same page. "But I might follow up with Jared Baker, see if maybe he's up for a job interview."

"Please don't."

She sighed. The ache in his voice reminded her the man was running on fumes as it was. She didn't need to add to his anxiety. "I'll let it rest. For today."

"Are you going to tell me about you and this Abernathy guy?"

She brushed his concern aside with a flick of her wrist. "Ancient history. Other than the visitation, I hadn't seen him since we graduated high school. Can't believe he became an insurance salesman, of all things," she added, wrinkling her nose. "Once upon a time, Bo thought he might be destined for a career in mixed martial arts."

Ben raised an interested brow. "He was into martial arts?"

She smirked, but a pang of sadness for the boy she once liked struck her hard. "Nope. He thought he'd learn some moves from one of those video sets they sell on late-night infomercials. I doubt he even made it through the first DVD."

"You two dated steady in high school," he said, completely ignoring any anecdotal color she might throw into the conversation.

"Neither of us expected it to go any further," she assured him. "Once he understood there wasn't a snowball's chance in Hades of me staying here in Pine Bluff and marrying him, he moved on to plan B."

"Which was mixed martial arts," he said, his lips twisting into a sneer.

Marlee shot him a look. "Bo Abernathy was the type of man who was always looking for a shortcut."

Ready to think of anything but Bo, she changed the subject. "Are you free this evening?"

"Yes."

"Interested in spending some time with me?"

"Yes."

She basked in the simplicity of his acceptance. No games. No beating around the bush. He gave her yes after yes. How could any woman resist? "I enjoy spending time with you, Sheriff," she murmured, leaning in for a kiss.

"That may be, but I believe you're operating on my time at the moment," a deep voice drawled from the doorway.

Chapter Fourteen

"Daddy!" Marlee gasped, her hand flying to her throat.

Ben jerked away from Marlee, but not fast enough to complete disentangle himself. "You're not the only one who's surprised," Henry Masters said, his expression foreboding.

But even faced with her father's obvious displeasure, Marlee simply rolled her eyes. "I sincerely doubt you're surprised," she said, dividing a look between her father and himself. "We had lunch together at the Daisy. God and half the town saw us. I'm amazed it took this long for word to make it back to you." She crossed her arms over her chest. "Your network may have some holes in it."

Henry sniffed at the implication. "Please. He wasn't simply giving you a lift home the other night. You all went out to the lake house. Why?"

Marlee shrugged, but for the first time since her father appeared, she avoided his gaze. "I haven't been out there since...Jeff."

Ben could tell she was trying to sound offhanded about it, but something rang hollow. Sure enough, she rolled her shoulders back and drew herself up, then faced Henry directly.

"I wanted to see what you'd done with the place."

"I see." The older man jingled the loose change in his pocket as he inspected them. "What did you think of it, Sheriff?"

Ben gave his answer a moment of thought. "I think it's a nice house with a sad history."

"Yes." Henry's voice was quiet.

Ben and Marlee exchanged a look. He turned back to Masters, ready to say something, anything, about his intentions toward the man's daughter, but he hadn't the first clue what they were. Marlee might still have plans to return to Atlanta at the first possible opportunity. This sizzle between them could be nothing more than heat. Something to add some spark to the time she was forced to stay here in Pine Bluff. How was he supposed to proclaim his feelings for her to her father when he hadn't the foggiest notion of whether she had feelings for him at all?

Henry spoke again, interrupting his thoughts. "Marlee, the Office of Bar Admissions sent a letter. Congratulations, you passed. You are officially a member of the Georgia Bar."

Marlee blinked. "You opened my mail?"

His eyebrows shot up. "You were okay with me opening the bills for your tuition," Henry said stiffly. "I didn't see how this should be any different."

"But—"

"Your mother and I believe this calls for a celebration. We'll be expecting you home for supper this evening."

Marlee looked like she'd just been hit by a speeding truck. "Yes, sir."

Ben darted a look in her direction, startled by her easy capitulation. Then she added a sunny smile that made the hairs on his arms stand on end.

"Would it be all right if I invited Ben to join us for supper?" she asked, all honeyed sweetness.

Her father rolled his eyes, apparently impervious to her myriad charms. Finally, he settled an assessing stare on Ben. "Perhaps the sheriff can join us another night. I've already invited Will to eat with us, and I hate to spring too many surprises on your poor mama."

"Oh."

The word slipped out of her, small and soft. Acquiescent. A syllable not at all worthy of Marlee. Hearing the note of uncertainty made his fingers curl into loose fists. He wanted to tell her he didn't care if he had to bring his own bucket of fried chicken to eat, he wasn't going to let her anywhere near Will Thomason without him.

Ben was still casting about for a way to insert himself into whatever setup Henry had going when Marlee swooped in and staged her own rescue.

"Well, Mama invited him when we were all at Mrs. Young's house, so I'm sure she won't mind. I'll call home and make sure Mrs. Franklin is aware we'll be five for supper."

"Good," Henry said with a terse nod. "Now you'd best get back to it. You have a lot to learn and not a lot of time to get up to speed." Done with her, he ze-roed in on Ben. "Sheriff, can I walk you out? I have a couple of questions."

Ben looked at Marlee, but she couldn't do much more than give him a shrug. "I'll text you later."

Nodding, he followed her father out of the con-ference room, feeling like a teenage boy about to be ejected from the parlor for kissing on the couch after curfew. The last thing he wanted to do was give Henry Masters the idea he could control any part of Ben's private life.

"Henry, I—"

The other man gave his head a hard shake, waved to Wendell's ever-vigilant secretary and led them out the door. Ben blinked against the glare of the harsh afternoon sunlight. Shielding his eyes, he drew to an abrupt halt and waited for Masters to realize he was no longer following. The older man was five steps away and still oblivious. Anxious to have his say, and afraid Henry might get himself whipped into a froth, Ben called out to him again—this time, using his most au-thoritative cop voice.

"Henry, stop."

Masters spun around, surprise lighting his face. He was a man accustomed to giving orders and watching people jump to do his bidding. But Ben had told him from the beginning he wouldn't be one of those people. Now was his time to prove it.

"I want to talk to you about your daughter," he said, closing the distance between them in two strides.

"She'll do everything in her power to get back to Atlanta," Henry informed him without hesitation.

"You plan on keeping her here," Ben countered.

The older man's eyes gleamed, and Ben had a hard time deciphering whether it was respect or challenge he saw there. "Yes, and I also hear tell you can't go back to Atlanta. At least, not if you don't want to end up in a pine box."

But the revelation didn't rattle Ben. His situation was hardly a secret within the agency. It would have surprised him more to discover Masters hadn't uncovered the reason for his decision to switch gears career-wise. "I have absolutely no doubt you think you have a good handle on me, but you don't."

Henry crossed his arms over his chest. "I'm sure you have some hidden depths, but I'm not particularly interested in plumbing them."

Ben stared hard at the shorter man. "You can tell me to back off, but the only person who can make me leave Marlee alone is Marlee herself."

"Why should I? You're the best enticement I have to keep her here," Henry pointed out.

"What do you want to ask me?"

For the first time since he'd met the man, Henry Masters looked uncertain. He pushed his hand through his thinning silver-gold hair, casting a wary glance at the door to Wendell's office. "Do you honestly think there's some deeper connection between my boy's death and these other men?"

Ben shouldn't have been surprised to discover Masters was up to speed on the suspicions Marlee had brought to him. Wendell had probably been on the phone to Henry the second he and Marlee left his office. Ben bristled momentarily but reminded himself Masters was actually Wingate's client and not Marlee or himself. Wendell had been under no obligation to keep their conversation confidential.

"I've taken it into consideration." Ben eyed Henry carefully and was thrown completely off balance when Henry Masters got misty-eyed on him.

"I thought Carolee... She never accepted it. I can't blame her," he said, his voice breaking as he rambled on. "It's unnatural to bury a child. Unbearable to think the boy you loved was so desperately unhappy he'd..." He trailed off, blinking furiously as he stared down at the patch of green lawn in front of Wendell's law offices.

At a loss for what to say, Ben fell back on the most general of platitudes, hoping to buy some time. "No one can ever truly understand what someone else is going through."

"He was happy," Henry insisted. "Well, not unhappy," he amended with a bitter laugh. "He was apprehensive about taking over the company one day, but he planned to have Marlee to help him, and he seemed to genuinely care for the Cabrera girl..."

Again, his words drifted away from him.

"It was such a shock." Clearing his throat, he gave his head a fierce shake. "Carolee kept insisting there was more to it, but the evidence—"

But the evidence. Those three words kept bouncing around Ben's head. "Yes," he said gruffly. "The evidence."

"But now these others. It can't be a coincidence," he stated firmly. He tossed another uncertain glance Ben's way. "Can it?"

"I don't think it is," Ben told him truthfully. "But it's not much to go on as far as theories go. There's a distinct lack of evidence."

"How can it be?" Masters wondered aloud. "The forensics all pointed to Jeff pulling the trigger himself."

Ben nodded, but his movements were made jerky by a flash of memory. Something Andre had once said to him as they sat on a dirty mattress in a dank southeastern Atlanta flophouse, waiting for members of their crew to return from what Ivan called a "retribution run." He remembered sitting there, staring at the water-stained ceiling and listening to his childhood friend spout some utter nonsense the gang leader believed about how a real man decides when it's his time to live or die.

"Maybe he did, but that doesn't necessarily mean he committed suicide."

"Now you're talking in riddles," Henry said derisively.

"No, I'm saying the cause and effect don't always align the way most people expect them to," Ben retorted. "Life isn't simple."

"So you're thinking someone coerced my son into putting a gun to his head and pulling the trigger?"

Until Henry Masters spoke the words out loud, Ben hadn't allowed himself to go there. But there it was.

Plain as day and damn-near impossible to prove. Unless they somehow caught the person responsible in the act. Thanks to Marlee, they had two possible suspects. One of them was coming to supper at Marlee's house.

"Exactly what I'm thinking," Ben confirmed with a short nod. "What time should I be at your house for supper tonight? I have a couple questions for Will Thomason."

Masters blinked twice, a look of resignation setting his features into a grim mask. "Six thirty for cocktails. We'll eat at seven."

"I CAN'T TELL you what a thrill it is to have so many handsome gentlemen at my table," Carolee said, her voice as high and breathy as a girl on her first phone call with a boy. She beamed as she offered Ben the mashed potatoes with a side of fluttering lashes. "Why, when Marlee told me you'd be joining us too, Sheriff, I ran right into the kitchen and told Mrs. Franklin nothing but Mother's English-rose china would do."

Marlee had to hand it to the man. He didn't look the least bit fazed by her mother's flirtation. "I can't tell you how happy I am for a good home-cooked meal, Mrs. Masters." Ben took the proffered dish from her. "And, please, call me Ben."

"Then you must call me Carolee," her mother parried.

"Mrs. Masters is fine," her father grumbled as he placed two slices of Mrs. Franklin's mouthwatering roast beef on his plate.

Marlee's impulse to laugh was stifled when the man

beside her spoke up. "And you should call me Will, Marlee."

With barely a glance, she swung a small serving platter his way. "Asparagus, Mr. Thomason?" she asked politely, emphasizing the use of his surname.

He didn't miss the hint. "Thank you, Ms. Masters," he said as he relieved her of the plate. "How are you enjoying your time with Wendell Wingate?"

His delivery was annoyingly congenial. He hadn't even noticed she'd been pointedly rude to him from the moment he walked through the door. Marlee cut him a sharp look. "How do you know I've been working with Mr. Wingate?"

The pause lasted a beat too long. Her question surprised him. The openness of his expressions made her feel more confident. She needed to gauge his reactions when she prodded him about the Sportsmen's Club and the parcels of land surrounding Sawtooth Lake.

"I was the one who suggested you spend time with him first," Thomason said, darting a puzzled look at Henry. "I guess your father didn't mention it."

She shook her head. "Nope. I showed up for my first day at the family business and got foisted off on the trusty family retainer."

Either her word choice or the flippancy captured her father's attention. For the first time since he herded them all from the front parlor into the dining room, Henry looked up from his plate. She saw the deep furrow between his brows and felt an instant stab of remorse. Her mother had always claimed Marlee and

Henry butted heads so much because they were too alike. Now, she saw her father's genuine befuddlement.

"'Foisted off'?"

"We thought working with Wendell would be the most logical place for you to start," Thomason cut in smoothly. The silence following his statement stretched a beat too long. Will rushed to fill it on her father's behalf. "Since the plan was for you to come into the administrative end of the business rather than production."

Henry cleared his throat. "Of course, those plans have changed, but it still seemed as good a place to start as any."

A sudden stillness filled the room as even her mother's incessant chatter died away. Marlee scanned her father's face for hints but found him as unreadable as ever. Beside her, Will Thomason tensed, though she had to hand it to him—he didn't let his consternation show. Still, she sensed him gathering his energy in tight, a snake coiling and set to strike.

Intrigued by her father's statement and the closely controlled reaction from the man everyone assumed to be his heir apparent, she placed her fork and knife on the edge of her plate and focused entirely on the man seated at the head of the table. "What do you mean?"

"What I said." Henry's response was sharp and direct. Stripped of his customary bluff and bluster. When all eyes swung to him expectantly, he shrugged their curiosity off. "We'll have to rethink our plans."

"Yes, speaking of, I have plans to order some new curtains for your room, Marlee. I was in there looking at them last night, and I realized it's been forever since I spruced the place up."

Marlee and Ben exchanged a meaningful look. There was one mystery solved. It had been her mother in her room after all. Regardless, she wasn't letting her guard down around Thomason anytime soon.

"I meant our long-range plans," Henry interrupted.

"*Our* long-range plans?" Marlee repeated, emphasizing his choice of pronoun.

"Yes." He fixed her with the same impatient but stubbornly entrenched expression he'd worn when drilling her on multiplication tables.

"You mean *your* plans," she said, choosing the more appropriate pronoun.

"Timber Masters is a family business. You are the last of the line. The company and all of our other interests will one day come to you." Her father didn't break eye contact. "It's my duty to see you are prepared."

Wendell had implied the exact same thing when they first met, but hearing her father lay it out there so bluntly came as a shock. At the opposite end of the table, her mother gasped. Snatching the creamy damask napkin from her lap, Carolee managed to cover her mouth but emitted a strangled sob.

"Mama," Marlee began, half rising in her chair, prepared to usher Carolee from the room if she couldn't rein in her emotions.

"Oh, for the love of—" Henry threw up his hands in surrender. "I dream of getting through one meal without hysterics."

Dropping back onto her seat, Marlee whirled on her

father. "Maybe your wife dreams of being able to get through one day without being reminded her only son is gone, but she doesn't have such luxuries."

"He was my son too," Henry fired back.

"Hey, now—" Holding the heavy china platter heaped with steaming slices of succulent beef, Ben tried to step into the fray. But he was no match for a Masters with a full head of steam. They ran over him from all directions.

"He never should have been out there. Jeffrey hated the lake house," Carolee fretted.

Marlee ignored him, choosing instead to gape at her mother. Her eyes widened at what she considered to be a fairly large exaggeration, but she couldn't be bothered with setting her mother straight. Not when she had her father to deal with.

Skipping right over Ben's pleading expression, she leaned into her anger as she spoke to her father. "And he was my brother. Now that we have all our roles assigned, I'd remind you Jeff never wanted to run the business. You bullied him into coming home."

"Bullied," Henry said, tossing his napkin onto the table with a harsh laugh. "I didn't bully either of you. I simply refused to foot the bill for you not doing your duty to the family." He fixed her with a cold stare. "You and your brother. All you talked about was escaping this town and shirking your responsibilities. You think I was clueless?" His voice shook as it rose in volume. "You don't want anything to do with the company your great-great-grandfather started, but you damn sure don't mind spending the money it makes."

"I had a job lined up, but you shot it down," she reminded him in a harsh whisper.

"A job with a man who—" Henry stopped abruptly, his gaze flying to the opposite end of the table and locking on his wife. "A job with a man who was only speaking to you because your name is Masters."

Awkward silence roared through the room.

Marlee dropped her gaze to her half-filled plate. They hadn't even loaded their plates with roast beef yet and supper was a complete wash. She took two deep breaths and tamped down the urge to howl at the injustice of it all. Everything. Jeff's death. Clint's too. The job in Atlanta she'd thought she wanted. The texts. The jovial jackass seated beside her. The man across the table. How would Ben have fit into the life she'd abandoned in Atlanta? After witnessing the Masters family in their full glory, would he even want anything to do with her?

Beside her plate, her muted phone buzzed once to indicate a new message had arrived. Marlee stiffened. Everyone who might text her was seated at this table. Including Will Thomason. Instinctively, she glanced at the man beside her, but he was carefully selecting a roll from the bread basket. Squirming in her seat, she ignored the tingle of fear that trickled down her spine and steeled her resolve to get to the bottom of his involvement in the land transaction. She'd deal with the texts later.

Wetting her parched lips, she looked up and found Ben staring straight at her, his dark eyes watchful. "Ben?"

"Yes, Marlee?" His gaze didn't waver from hers despite her mother's sniffling and her father's grumbles of displeasure.

"May I have the roast beef, please?"

Still holding her gaze, he offered the platter to her. She took it in both hands then placed it on the table between herself and Will Thomason. Gesturing for their guest to help himself first, she watched as he speared a slice, then served herself and her mother. The potatoes finished making the rounds as well.

Proving her patience and, yes, stubbornness were indeed equal to her father's, she waited until Will had cut off a bite of roast and popped it into his mouth before starting her interrogation. "As president of the Sawtooth Lake Sportsmen's Club, what do you think about losing nearly half your membership in the last year?"

BEN WOULD BE lying if he said he didn't enjoy watching Will Thomason sputter and spin his wheels throughout Marlee's killer line of questioning. She pressed him about how he'd met each of the members, how he'd come to step into the position of president after her brother's death, what all the job entailed. She carried the whole interrogation out while her mother sat sniffling on one end of the table and her father repeatedly tried to intercede from the other. Through it all, Marlee remained utterly unflappable, her performance even more breathtaking than the woman herself.

Sure, some of her angles of attack were a bit awkward and some of her phrasing too close-ended, but he didn't interrupt or try to correct her course. He'd had years of training on how to get the most out of a suspect. She might be newly admitted to the bar, but she cross-examined the squirming man with aplomb. She had the right instincts. The rest would come with time and experience.

Carolee Masters drained her wineglass early in the meal, but no one leaped to fill it for her. By the time Marlee picked up her phone and rose to start clearing plates, Ben almost felt sorry for the poor woman. When Mrs. Masters started to rise too, he set his napkin aside and waved her back into her chair. "No, ma'am. Let me help."

Henry and Will stayed seated, their stunned expressions confirming his suspicion they'd never made such an offer in their lives. Feeling fairly smug for a man carrying a stack of delicate china through the swinging door leading to a surprisingly modern chef's kitchen, he placed the plates he'd collected on the counter next to Marlee's.

"You were magnificent in there," he said quietly.

"I didn't get anything out of him," she said with a huff of disappointment.

"I think you did," he argued.

She lifted her eyes to meet his. "Yeah?"

"Yeah. I think we can agree Will Thomason is ambitious and opportunistic." He lifted his chin. "Check your message."

She closed her eyes for a moment, then beamed the smile to unlock the phone.

No one believes you were with Sheriff Kinsella. You must be paying the man to cover for you.

"Crap," he whispered as Marlee seemed to deflate.

"I could have sworn those texts came from Will. There's something about the way he talks to me." She gave a shudder. "But there's no way he could have unless he schedules them to come at different times. How could he know what I was doing ahead of time, though?"

He had no answer for her. Placing one hand on her shoulder, he rubbed gently as they both read the message again. "Whoever it is, their spelling and punctuation have improved," she said with a forced laugh that fell flat.

He was about to tell her not to fake it with him when something about her observation struck a chord. "Wait. Go back through the others."

Marlee did as he asked, scrolling back to the message she'd received right after she'd returned to town. By the time they got to the last few, one thing became glaringly obvious. This was one case where punctuation counted.

Ben read the message over her shoulder, then pulled out his own phone. He turned away as the call connected. "Mike? I want you to call Judge Warner and ask for a warrant for all electronic devices belonging to Bo or Kayla Abernathy. Then call up to Albany and tell them we need a tech guy down here ASAP."

"Kayla Abernathy?" Marlee asked when he ended the call. "Why?"

"Jealousy?" He shrugged. "She'd have access to his

phone or computer or whatever he was using. Only a handful of people know you gave a statement about us being together last night."

Their gazes locked. "I guess."

"He was trying to talk to you. She was trying to scare you away."

"It almost worked."

"God, I hope not." He sighed, then ran a hand over her hair. "We can talk about this later, but for now, we'd better get back." He cast about the kitchen. "You said something about dessert?"

Nodding, she headed for the oven, snagging a dish towel from the counter along the way. "Grab the ice cream from the freezer."

Ben did his best to keep his gaze aboveboard when she bent, protecting her hands with the towel so she could extract a covered dish from the rack. She set it on the stovetop, then tossed the towel over her shoulder. "Ta-da! Peach cobbler."

"Peach cobbler and a beautiful woman," he said as he pulled a container of ice cream from the freezer. "Proof there is still good in the world."

Chapter Fifteen

The moment they were settled in his car, Marlee turned to him. "Tell me about your parents."

The request startled him. Ben wrapped his hands around the steering wheel and drew in a deep breath, then let it go in a steady stream.

"Come on. You've witnessed mine in all their glory," she cajoled.

He plugged the key into the ignition and cranked the engine, giving it some gas so it roared to life. "Let's take a drive," he said gruffly.

If he was going to tell her a story about a man falling for a girl so far out of his reach that it had ruined him, he sure as hell wasn't going to do it while parked in front of the family mansion.

Without giving it much thought, he wheeled the car around and headed for the highway. "My dad played basketball," he said, beginning at what he considered the man's downfall. "Mostly neighborhood stuff, youth groups, wherever he could." He drummed his fingers on the wheel. "I'm told he was good. So good people from the private high schools came scouting around, looking to recruit some raw talent to add to their rosters."

He didn't bother glancing over at her as he headed down the road that would take them out of the town she would essentially run one day. "My grandmother was ecstatic. All she wanted was for her son to get a good education and get out of the neighborhood. Peachtree Academy was supposed to be the answer to her prayers."

When he fell silent for a moment, she pushed. "What happened?"

"He fell for the Homecoming Queen," he answered without missing a beat. "I guess she was the queen of everything. Blond, blue-eyed, the girl who had everything." He chanced a sidelong look at her. "No telling what she saw in him, exactly. Maybe she thought dating a guy from the 'hood was exotic or something. Probably nothing more than teenage rebellion." He shook his head in disgust. "In the end, she got pregnant and her parents kicked her out."

"Whoa." Instinctively, he let off the gas, but another peek at Marlee told him she wasn't commenting on his driving. "She must have been so scared."

Both annoyed and touched by her compassion for the mother he barely knew, he let the truck coast as they approached the lake road. "Keep going or turn off?"

If Marlee thought the question had two meanings, she didn't let on. She simply gestured to the narrow lane and said, "Go on."

They bumped along the lake road for a minute before Marlee said, "Tell me."

He shrugged. "There isn't a lot more to tell. They

moved in with my grandmother. If my mother was scared of anything, it was the neighborhood. It was a fairly hopeless place. Lots of drugs. More than our fair share of thugs to go with them." The truck down-shifted to a crawl as he revealed the rest of the story. "Three weeks after I was born, my mother took off. She hadn't lost touch with her old friends. One of them picked her up and drove her back to her parents' house, where I can only assume there was a joyful, mixed baby–free reunion."

"And your dad? He didn't try to go after her?"

He gave a bitter laugh. "My dad. He was still a true believer in those days, I guess. He thought her parents had taken her, so he hitched a ride up to Buckhead and tried to bust her out."

He heard Marlee's sharp intake of breath and let the pause stretch for a moment. "What happened to him?"

"He served ten years for criminal trespass, felony damage to property, kidnapping a person over fourteen years of age," he reported flatly.

"You're kidding me."

He quelled her outrage with a hard look. "Do you think I'm kidding?"

"No, you're not," she said in a horrified whisper.

He could feel her searching look but refused to glance at her. He couldn't let her see the shame and degradation he felt on behalf of his grandmother, a steady, God-fearing woman who'd never done anything to deserve the hardships life piled on her.

"What happened to your parents?"

He shrugged then, out of habit more than necessity, and flipped the signal on to indicate the turn into the drive. "My mother went off to college at Auburn. She couldn't stay anywhere local because *everyone* knew," he said dryly. "She ended up marrying a guy from Mobile."

"And you have never heard from her?"

"I tried to contact her when I was seventeen. I'd signed up for the marines and wanted her to see I wasn't some loser. Wanted to tell her I was going to serve my country and she should be proud of the mutt she'd abandoned."

"Ben—"

Rather than listen to her give him the pep talk he'd needed then but didn't need anymore, he pressed on with his story. "My dad fell in with a gang while he was inside, continued with them when he got out. My grandmother refused to take the money he made dealing, so we pretty much had nothing. She passed away right after I finished boot camp. Breast cancer."

"What happened to your dad?"

"Oh, he was already dead. Got popped when a drop went south on him. I was a sophomore in high school. The guys he ran with tried to recruit me. Said taking care of Big Benji's family was the least they could do, but my grandmother wouldn't let them come anywhere near me."

"Big Benji," she repeated. "You were named for him."

He nodded. "The last in a long line of losers." He coasted on the approach to the house, the tires crunching on loose gravel as they rolled to a stop. "I'm not even sure why I drove us out here."

Marlee stared bleakly at the house where her brother had died. "Because you were telling me about the mess you lived through, and this is where my mess started." She gestured to the house, her voice quiet and reflective. "This was where Jeff and I cooked up the plan for me to go to law school. He was going to play the game until he took full control of the company, then sell out." She bit her lower lip and let it go when she exhaled. "He didn't want to be like Daddy, and he wasn't." When she looked over at him, her eyes gleamed with unshed tears. "I am."

"Why do you say so?"

She motioned to the house, then to the woods around them. "I can't let it go. Any of it. Jeff's death, this land, the business. I haven't figured out how I'm going to handle it, but I can tell you I won't be selling out. I don't want to live here in Pine Bluff and be the queen of all things Masters, but I won't—I can't—let anyone else do it."

Ben tightened his grip on the steering wheel until his knuckles shone pale against his skin. "I can't let this go any further between us. I won't go down the same path as my father."

"You're afraid getting involved with me will turn you into a gangbanger who deals drugs?"

"I refuse to be a cliché. Nothing good can come out of a guy like me reaching for a woman like you."

"That's the second time you've tried to pigeonhole me," she said, her voice soft and dangerous. "What have I shown you to make you think I think I'm better than you?"

He shook his head, at a complete loss but unable to let go of his convictions too easily. What if he was only seeing what he wanted to see in her? What if she was only putting on a show? Or worse, what if he gave her everything he had and she decided he wasn't what she wanted? After all, his mother had chosen his father once upon a time, but it didn't take long for her to change her mind.

"Forget my looks or whatever," she implored. "Forget who my father is, and pretend my last name is Smith. Would you want to be with me?"

He laughed, but this time there was nothing harsh about it. He laughed because the notion of imagining her in any other way was absurd. She was who she was because she was Marlee Masters of Masters County, Georgia. Her blonde beauty queen looks drew a man in, but she was so much more than an attractive package. Marlee was smart, funny, friendly and, yes, a bit daring. Even then, mere adjectives failed to capture the essence of her. Because above all else, Marlee was genuine. A real person with foibles and fancies but also with feelings. Deep feelings she didn't show to just anyone. But for some reason, she showed them to him, and he'd be damned if he could figure out why.

"It's not a matter of wanting, Marlee," he said at last. "I want to be with you. Any man with half a brain would, and I have a whole brain. But I can't help but wonder why you keep hanging around me. You can have your pick of men. Why me? What do you want from me?"

For a moment, she looked ready to toss out one of her flippant retorts, but she didn't. Instead, she pressed her lips tight and swallowed hard, then made such intense eye contact with him he felt the urge to draw back.

"Why you?"

Arrested by her, he could only nod in response.

"I could give you a handful of reasons, but to even the playing field, I will skip your looks, the sexy uniform and all other superficial stuff." She stared deep into his eyes, needing to be sure her point hit home. "But don't for one minute think all those things don't work in your favor as well, because they do."

"Noted."

"My father may be a pain in the behind in a lot of ways, Ben, but there's one thing he is and has always been. A man of integrity. As such, he looks for the same in others. He sees what I see in you. A stand-up guy. Someone who will do anything to do the right thing."

"You don't know me."

"Maybe I don't know everything about you, but I think we understand one another. I feel…comfortable with you."

He gave a husky laugh. "The ringing endorsement every guy hopes for."

She could only answer that with a wan smile. "I know, but maybe you'll believe me when I tell you it's a better compliment than it sounds?"

"I believe you."

Her smile widened. "And that, right there. You have a sort of…self-assurance that's compelling."

"You're saying I'm cocky?" he teased.

She shook her head with vehemence. "No. Will is cocky. You're confident. Totally different things."

"Will," Ben said, his inflection dripping with derision.

"I know," she said with a laugh. "I get the feeling Henry was making two points at once in inviting Will tonight." She raised one finger. "To make it absolutely clear to him and everyone else that I am the only person who would be inheriting Timber Masters and everything that goes with it." She took a shuddering breath, reality sinking in. "Two, that all of Will's jostling and positioning himself beside Henry was for nothing. Unless, of course, he decides to marry me."

"Over my dead body," Ben growled.

She tilted her head to the side, then smiled wide and bright. If he had to testify, Ben would swear the sun reappeared in the darkening sky. "So, can you see how the whole 'I can't be involved with you but any other man would have to step over my dead body to get you' thing might be confusing to me?"

"Are you staying or are you going, Marlee?" he asked, his eyes boring into her. "Because Atlanta… Atlanta is not an option for me. It never will be."

"You probably feel the same way about Atlanta as I do about Pine Bluff—"

"No. It's not the same." He grasped both her hands in his and waited until he was sure he had her full attention. "I can never go back to Atlanta because I made a deal in exchange for my life."

"What?"

"I was undercover. Things went bad. Really bad. I crossed a man named Ivan Jones. A really bad dude. The only way I could get out alive was to leave and promise to never come back." He squeezed her hands. "Trust me, the people who work for him are watching."

"How do you know?"

"They send messages every now and then, make it clear they're keeping tabs on where I am and what I'm doing."

"Can't the DEA do anything?"

His expression hardened. "Maybe, but they won't. They let me go when my cover was blown."

"They can't—"

"Yes, they could. Trust me. I broke rules. Most agents who live deep undercover do. It comes back to bite some of us. In my case, they used it for cause."

"But—"

Indignation fired the blue flame in her eyes. He released her hand and pressed his fingertip to her lips. "It's done, Marlee. I've moved on." He gave a laugh, but it sounded tight. "I moved here. The one place you can't stand to be."

"Ben, if it means being with you—"

Whatever she said was cut off by the crackle of the police radio on his dash. "Sheriff? Do you read me?"

It was Lori calling for him, and the jerky cadence of her call told him something was wrong. He snatched the mic from the clip. "Read."

"Can you… I need you to come here. We, uh, we have a situation."

Ben scrubbed his face with the palm of his hand. "What kind of a situation?"

"Uh, I went to the Abernathys' to get their computers and stuff. Mrs. Abernathy tried to refuse to give them up—"

"Did Mike get the warrant?"

"Yes. We had it, and we got the stuff," Lori assured him. "But Mrs. Abernathy is making a stink."

"What kind of stink?" he asked, rubbing his forehead.

"She's telling all the neighbors you're sleeping with Marlee Masters and that's why she hasn't been arrested for murdering her brother, Clint Young and Bo Abernathy."

WHILE BEN DEALT with the widow Abernathy and her accusations, Marlee cornered her father. She needed answers, and if there was anyone in this town with answers, it would be her father. Thankfully, Will Thomason was nowhere in sight when she got home.

"How did Bo make all his money?" She hadn't bothered to knock on Henry's office door. "I mean, the insurance business is good and all, but his folks didn't have a pot of money. How could he have amassed enough to even buy into the insurance agency?"

Her father opened his hands. "How am I to guess?"

"I understand Mr. Behrend's retired, but they don't hand over an insurance agency to anyone who applies," she continued, pushing away from the door and making her way to the guest chair in front of his antique desk. "When did he get a license? Last I heard, he got his diploma and nothing more. No college, no plans. When we graduated, he had a job changing oil at Hewes Brothers garage. How does Bo Abernathy go from nothing to building a house on the lake?"

"Believe it or not, I don't make a habit of prying into other people's business."

Switching tactics, she nudged a stack of file folders perched on the edge of his desk. "How about Will Thomason? Where'd he come from?"

"I believe his people hail from the Marietta area."

"I didn't mean his family," Marlee said, pinning him with a stare. "How did a guy who didn't even grow up here end up next in line for Jeff's job?"

"He's not next in line for Jeff's job," Henry corrected. "You are."

"You realize he doesn't think so," she said, smirking as she recalled the look on Will's face at dinner. "He's pretty sure he can make you change your mind."

"Then he's mistaken," her father said, folding his hands in front of him.

"I have no intention of marrying him so he can run the family business."

"I won't insult you by pretending the thought hadn't crossed my mind, but I think you've made it clear your interests lie elsewhere."

"How did he end up here?" she persisted. "Most of your managers and foremen are homegrown." She studied her father closely. "How did this guy make it into the inner circle?"

"Through your brother."

"Jeff?" She couldn't mask her surprise. It was hard to imagine her quiet, studious brother being friends with Will Thomason. "Wow."

"I don't think they were close friends," Henry conceded, following the trail of her thoughts easily enough. "Will graduated from UGA a couple years ahead of Jeff. I believe they were in the same fraternity. When he applied for a foreman's position, Jeff confirmed Will had indeed graduated from the Warnell School of Forestry."

"He wanted to be a mill foreman?"

"He didn't want to work for one of the large paper conglomerates," he corrected, sitting up straighter in his leather executive chair. "Believe it or not, lead positions at Timber Masters are highly sought after. We can offer hands-on experience the larger companies cannot."

"As long as you're willing to work at a company with limited opportunity for advancement," she added. "I'm not trying to give offense, Daddy," she said in a rush. "I'm only wondering why a man with other options would choose to climb a ladder with such a low ceiling."

Henry shrugged, slightly mollified but clearly still miffed. "He was unhappy in his previous position and didn't want to go to work for the big boys. With everything happening around here, I was getting dragged into town business more and more. Jeff seemed to trust him, so I was happy to take him."

"So he came here right about the time the whole DEA thing was happening," she concluded.

Henry nodded.

"You don't find the timing odd? That someone would want to move into the area when all the unsavory stuff was happening around here?"

This time, her father gave no more than a jerky shrug. "When you put it in those terms…" He ran his hand over his face again, and her heart slammed into her breastbone. Here, with the light from the desk lamp casting dark shadows across his face, her father looked haggard. Old. For the first time ever, she realized he'd been carrying the weight of their whole world on his shoulders. Her brother's death, her mother's grief and inability to cope, her unwillingness to come home to help.

"It does seem odd the Abernathy boy would fall into such a plum position," he said with a sigh. "I guess… I'm not sure. It's been such a strange time."

Marlee's stomach knotted. The urge to reach across the desk and squeeze his hand had her balling her fingers into a fist. They didn't have a touchy-feely relationship.

"I would think there would have to have been some sort of influence exerted," she mused.

"Excuse me?" Henry pulled himself from his ruminations.

"He couldn't walk in off the street and take over an agency. There are licenses to be obtained, courses to pass," she said, gesturing impatiently. "Either someone with a good deal of money or influence placed him there.

"Bo was always smart in a sly sort of way," Marlee continued quietly. Her father let out a short laugh, and she couldn't suppress a rueful chuckle herself. "Bright but lazy." A surge of power rushed through her as the bulb went on in her brain. "I told Ben how Bo loved shortcuts. What if he had someone backing him? Someone with some money—"

"Who?" Henry interrupted. "His parents couldn't hang on to two nickels at the same time."

"Maybe he was making some extra money on the side," she postulated. "And Will. How was he able to buy in to the club on a foreman's salary?"

Henry blew out a gusty breath. "I can't say. I assumed he had some family money. He has all sorts of connections in Atlanta. Worked for a sort of a brokerage place. Perhaps he made his money there?"

"And then moved to the sticks to oversee second shift at a lumber mill?" She shook her head. "What was the name of this firm?"

Henry rolled his eyes heavenward, then shrugged again. "I honestly don't recall. I can check his personnel record."

Marlee nodded as she stood. "Yeah. Let's do that first thing. I want to poke around a bit, see if I can follow the paper trail on the land sale."

Her father rose too. "The land sale? Why?"

"Wendell said the firm who acquired the land was a real estate holding company. I want to see who they contracted with as the developer, and who is actually leasing the land to Will, Bo and Jared Baker."

"It seems odd we haven't heard one word from Jared Baker since all this started," Henry commented. "Then again, he's mainly in contact with Will."

Marlee paused in the open doorway to look back at her father. "Another coincidence." She bit her lip and shook her head. "This place is lousy with them."

"Crystal Forest Corporation," Wendell said as he leafed through a file. They'd all gathered at the attorney's offices bright and early. Even Ben. "The name of the company who actually owns the land at the moment is Crystal Forest Corporation," he clarified. "After Henry called last night, I called in a couple of favors from more technologically adept friends, and they chased it down."

"I thought you said it was some law firm acting on behalf of a trust," Ben chimed in, his confusion evident.

"But the original sale was actually made to White, Pinkman, et al., correct?" Marlee's forehead puckered in a way her mother would surely have chastised.

"Yes. It has gone through a couple more transfers and has now landed with this Crystal Forest Corporation," Wendell confirmed.

"Why does that sound familiar to me?" Henry wondered aloud.

"Didn't Will Thomason work there prior to coming to Timber Masters?" Marlee scrambled to pull the personnel file she'd shoved into her leather tote free. "I read it in here somewhere."

"Crystal Forest," Ben repeated, his eyes focused on something beyond her shoulder. He let out a snort, then said, "No way."

An odd note in his tone caught her attention. "What?"

He dropped his gaze to the polished conference table, but his voice was still distracted when he shifted to sit up taller. "Nothing… The, uh, name struck me."

"Struck you how?" she pressed.

Ben looked up and straight into her eyes. "Crystal meth," he said flatly.

Her jaw dropped as the pieces began to fall into place, but one bit of his conjecture didn't quite fit. "But how would Jeff tie in?" When Ben leveled an unblinking look at her, she shook her head vehemently. "My brother would never get involved in the drug trade."

"People do things they may not want their family—"

"No." She all but spat the word at him as she shot from her chair. "Not Jeff."

"Marlee." Ben rose as well, but she backed away.

"No!" All three men jerked when she shouted the denial. Her voice trembled with rage. "Of all people, you should know."

"Why me 'of all people'?" Ben's voice rose as he circled the end of the table, moving steadily toward her with his ridiculous assumptions.

"Why did you join the military, Ben? What made you want a career with the DEA?" Oblivious to Wendell and her father, she tipped her chin up. "Jeff wasn't the bad guy in this scenario," she hissed. "He was a guy like you—the kid whose parent was half out of it most of the time."

Henry started to rise from his chair. "Now, wait a—"

But Marlee was on a roll, and she wasn't stopping until she knocked over every rock in her path. "You're assuming my mother took up popping pills when my brother passed, but that isn't the case. She's been up and down her whole life—"

"Marlee Kathleen—"

She ignored her father's attempt to interject. "Pour some booze on top and stir in a husband who cared more about his kingdom than he did about his family—"

"Enough!" Henry Masters roared, inserting himself between Marlee and Ben.

The three of them stood in a breathless triangle, tempers high and eyes blazing as they each tried to rein it in.

"I can assure you all Jeffrey was not involved in the drug business." Wendell's voice floated up from behind them, calm and gentle as a spring breeze.

Ben shot the older man a skeptical glance. "How can you be certain?"

"Because I was the one who helped him clean up the mess it left. He loathed what was happening around here." Wendell nodded, then flipped open one of the many files stacked in front of him and hit Marlee with a hard stare. "Now, if you're done bickering amongst yourselves, I can also tell you the Baker Law Firm has handled each of the transactions."

"There's something else," Henry insisted. He ran his hand through his gray-blond hair, then looked directly at Ben. "Jared Baker was the one who gave me your name for the sheriff's job."

Silence fell over the room like a shroud.

Wendell flattened his palms on the polished table. "I would say we seem to have two persons of interest at this point."

Chapter Sixteen

"When we get in there, let me do the talking," Marlee said as they approached the offices of the Baker Law Firm. Her father looked as startled by the demand as she felt. "Right now, we only need to confirm how this all came about, but I have a gut feeling."

Henry frowned at her. "What kind of gut feeling?"

"I'm not entirely sure. Trust me on this?"

He eyed her closely for a long minute, then nodded his assent. Marlee tried her best not to preen as she gestured to the door, but her father's approbation was more rewarding than she had ever expected. "Shall we?"

"Let's get this over with," Henry said impatiently.

Within minutes, they were seated in a sleekly appointed conference room. Marlee mumbled her thanks for the bottle of water placed in front of her by the efficient woman who'd shown them into the room, then took a moment to drink in the industrial-chic surroundings. The exposed brick and conduit made the firm feel hip and edgy to her. Most of the big downtown firms matched their chrome-and-steel furnishings to the skyscrapers housing them or went for a more staid, conservative decor. They screamed establishment. She saw the distressed oak conference table for exactly what it was—set dressing.

"Hello." Jared Baker strode into the room, a broad welcoming smile on his face and his hand outstretched. He shook with her father first, then worked his way around to her. She tried not to bristle at being placed at the bottom of the implied pecking order as he shook her hand. "We finally have a chance to meet." He greeted her smoothly, gesturing for them all to take their seats again. "What can I help you with today?"

Marlee made an effort to relax her shoulders as she maintained eye contact with Baker. "A couple years ago, you handled a land purchase for one of your clients." She flipped open her portfolio and consulted the photocopied page. "Crystal Forest Corporation?"

Jared nodded. "Sounds familiar."

"It ought to. You bought into a leasehold with them." She drew out a sheet of paper with the names of the Sawtooth Lake Sportsmen's Club members listed in a neat column. "We're making an offer to buy the land back."

The other attorney's smile faded by a watt or two. "Excuse me?"

"The land. It's been in my family for generations, and other than setting up a club which has only drawn yourself and people from local families—" she inclined her head "—it can't hold much meaning for your client. I'm sure the Sawtooth Lake property is just another parcel in a vast array of holdings," she continued.

"We would agree to honor the existing leaseholds, of course. Including your own."

Baker sat back in his seat, his elbows propped on the arms of his chair. "Hmm." He steepled his fingers beneath his bottom lip, giving the notion his full consideration. "Well, I'm not entirely certain my client would be interested in selling."

"We'd be willing to pay fair market value for the acreage, plus cover any closing costs or other expenses related to the sale." She saw her father stiffen, but thankfully, he remained silent. She flipped to a page in her portfolio, then extracted a proposal she'd typed up and printed on a sheet of Timber Masters letterhead she'd swiped from Wendell's offices. "Here's our offer, but I'm afraid we have a ticking clock on this. The assets we have liquified need to be reinvested by Friday, which means we only have about forty-eight hours to come to an agreement."

"Forty-eight hours?" Jared sat up straighter. "So quick."

"Looking back at the paperwork from the original sale, your clients moved fairly quickly when they decided to invest their money in the property." She leaned in and dropped her voice to a more confidential level. "We're working with an excess of cash on the balance sheet at the moment. Best to keep the money moving. Don't you agree?"

They locked gazes, and a shiver ran down her spine. The look he gave her was speculative but admiring. But rather than feeling gratified by his appreciative stare, Marlee had to curl her toes in her smart black pumps in order to keep from squirming in her chair. She waited without moving a muscle until he picked up the sheet she'd slid across the slick table and took in the numbers. One corner of his mouth twitched upward. It was a tell, but she had no idea if it meant something good or bad.

"I'll make a call today."

"Wonderful." Marlee flipped her portfolio closed and gripped the arms of the chair as she rose, trying to keep the tremors she was feeling on the inside. "We look forward to hearing from you." She thrust her hand across the table, and Jared Baker shook it, an amused gleam in his eyes.

"You've got a go-getter, Henry. I'm sad I couldn't take her on."

Disgusted, Marlee strode from the conference room, leaving the men to their backslapping and self-congratulations. She couldn't waste time on them now. She needed to get back to Pine Bluff. The trap had been set. Now they had to wait to see which creepy-crawly came out of the woods to take the bait.

"Hello," Ben said when she opened the door to the lake house to admit him.

"Hey." She rose up onto her tiptoes to brush a kiss to his cheek. "Come in."

Sweeping a hand in exaggerated welcome, she moved back to open the door wider. He took the opportunity to peer past her into the house. Part of him was surprised he didn't find Wendell and Henry waiting with her. Another part of him was glad they'd finally be alone. He pulled off the broad-brimmed trooper's hat and stepped through the door.

"I haven't gotten any more text messages," she told him.

"Kayla Abernathy confessed to sending the last few," he informed her. "The tech found the program on Bo's laptop, and, well, you can press charges if you want."

Marlee shook her head. "I don't want to add to her grief."

An awkward silence stretched between them. Ben noted that it was the first time they'd encountered the phenomenon and did his level best to push through it. "I hear you and your father took a trip to Atlanta today," he said, fidgeting with the brim of his hat in his hands as he strolled through the large open-concept living area.

"Yes."

"I wish you would have waited," he grumbled.

"Waited for what?" she pushed. "You can't go there. Besides, what we did today might not even have a direct bearing on the cases you're looking at."

"*We're* looking at," he corrected. He stared directly into those electric-blue eyes. "You're the one who dragged me into this whole thing," he reminded her.

"I did." Her tone was gentle. Conciliatory. He wasn't buying it for a minute.

"So, what did you find out?"

"Nothing specific. I made an offer to buy back the land."

He did a double take. "What?"

"I have no idea if whoever is behind this Crystal Forest land deal will go for it, but it seemed worth a try. If I can recover my family's land... It was worth a try. And it worked. We had a signed agreement in my inbox by the time we got back."

"Congratulations."

"Mostly I wanted to see Jared Baker's face when he saw who his visitors were. He's had dealings with both my father and me. He has about ten fingers in our pie, and I need to figure out why."

"I can tell you why," he said, his voice flat.

"You can?"

"I spoke to one of my friends at the agency today." He gestured toward the sofa. "I think we should sit down."

"I don't care for the sound of this." They sat, their knees briefly touching as he angled toward her. "Why do I need to be sitting down?"

"The suggestion was more for me than for you." He expelled a long breath. "I asked about Crystal Forest or if they had knowledge of any jokers using the *Breaking Bad* names as pseudonyms. The conversation came around to Ivan Jones—"

"The guy who's been after you?" she asked, her voice kicking up an octave. "I thought he was in jail now."

Ben gave a rough snort of laughter. "Jail doesn't mean much to guys like Ivan."

"You're scaring me."

He shook his head. "No need to be scared."

"If you say so."

"I do." He took the opportunity to give her hand a reassuring squeeze. "Crystal Forest is a shell company. They own a lot of smaller businesses they use to launder money. It belonged to Ivan."

"What?" Her eyes widened, then narrowed. "Oh, my God. Forget fingers. This guy is in up to his elbows."

"That's not all."

"Of course not."

He nodded, smiling at her ability to be snarky despite the gravity of their situation. "Ivan and his associates haven't forgotten what the agency did to his business in this area."

"I bet they haven't."

His mouth tightened, and he forced himself to breathe in through his nose before dropping the bigger bombshells on her. "According to my source, Jared Baker was Ivan Jones's attorney of record."

"Really?"

"There's more."

Marlee squeezed her eyes shut. "Stop saying that. I'm not sure how much more I can take."

"Ivan Jones was jumped by some other prisoners about a month ago and beaten into a coma. He died three days ago."

"He's dead?"

He nodded and she bit her bottom lip, white teeth sinking into the tender flesh as she processed the information and the myriad implications.

At last, she released it with a gusty sigh. "Good."

Her single word response to news with the power to alter the course of his whole life coaxed a laugh from him. "Yeah. Good." He ran a hand over his face. "The man was pure evil. He used to do all sorts of messed-up stuff. Andre told me about this time he made a guy…" He stalled as the story his friend told him in a flophouse a lifetime ago played out in his head.

"What?"

"Why didn't I think of it?"

Ben must have stared into space a minute too long, because Marlee waved a hand in front of his unseeing gaze to get his attention.

"Think of what? Ben? Speak. What are you thinking?"

But he was too busy fitting puzzle pieces into place to let his concentration be broken. "Ivan. Ivan owned Crystal Forest. Will worked for Ivan at Crystal Forest. It was Ivan."

"What was Ivan? How can anything be Ivan?"

"Because everything circles back to that sadistic jackass," he growled.

"But Ben—"

He cut her off before she tried to apply anything as useful as logic to the way Ivan Jones had operated. "Ivan didn't like to get his hands dirty, but he liked to mess with people's heads. One of his favorite things to do was to force people to play Russian roulette."

"What? How?" she asked, her brow crinkling.

He was trying to formulate how to explain when the cabin door flew open and Henry Masters stumbled in.

"I got a voice message from Will Thomason. He's over at his cabin now, but there's something off."

The words were barely out of his mouth when two

nearly simultaneous gunshots rang out. Ben and Marlee leaped to their feet, and Henry swung toward the lake. A moment later, the reverberation of a third shot echoed across the still water, but rather than taking cover, Henry Masters set out for his car.

Ben pushed past Marlee and took off after her father. "No, don't!" he shouted as he ran out the door.

He was halfway down the steps when he heard footfalls slapping the deck behind him. "Get back inside," he yelled over his shoulder, sprinting for the Suburban. The engine roared to life, but Henry hadn't shut the driver's door. "No," he barked, reaching into the car and practically dragging the older man from the seat. He switched off the ignition. "What the hell do you think you're doing?"

"We can't—" Henry's voice broke as he struggled in Ben's grip. "I can't let him do it. No more. No more."

The man spoke in a half rant, half sob, but Ben didn't need a translator to understand what he was trying to say. "You think Thomason was planning to kill himself out here tonight?"

"How am I supposed to know?" Henry bellowed. "I can't... Not another one."

Still gripping Henry by the arms, he shoved him toward his county-issued SUV. Opening the rear door, he pushed the older man in. "We're going. I'll take you," he promised. If he convinced the man to get in the back seat, he wouldn't be able to get out without someone to open the door from the outside.

After closing Henry in, he reached for the driver's door and swept the area for Marlee, praying she'd heeded his direction to go back into the house. The second he slid into the seat, he realized he'd given Marlee Masters too much credit when it came to common sense, because she was planted squarely in the passenger seat of his car.

"Marlee, we don't have time—"

She strapped into her seatbelt, then fixed him with the same stubborn glare he'd gotten from her father. "Then maybe you should stop yapping and start driving, Sheriff."

Less than a minute later, they were back on the lake road. Ben floored the accelerator. Marlee clung to the handle above the door as they sped down the rutted lane cutting through dense forest, but he didn't dare let up. "Grab the mic. Call for backup. Shots fired at Thomason lake house. Officer en route, approaching destination." Marlee dutifully repeated him verbatim. "I'll wait for backup as long as I can, but I need to assess the situation. Request backup from any Prescott County patrols in the area."

She'd hardly gotten the last part out when Ben stomped on the brakes and the SUV skidded to a halt outside the clearing where Will Thomason's house sat. It was a prefabricated home but had the look of a traditional log cabin. One room, or possibly two smaller areas. It was situated in the center of a heavily wooded lot, away from the lakeshore.

Ben squinted through the windshield, trying to make out the details of any entrances and exits in the lowering gloom of the evening storm. The back door had nothing but four wooden steps leading to it, but the entire width of the front had a deck. A pair of camp chairs sat at one end. The rest was bare. Apparently, Thomason wasn't big on homey touches. The second he reached for his door handle, Marlee went for hers. "No," he barked.

"But you can't go in there alone. It will take at least fifteen minutes for backup to get out here," she argued.

"You aren't going in there," he growled.

Henry Masters cleared his throat but spoke in a voice barely louder than a whisper. "Keep it down. Sound carries out here."

"I need you both to stay here," Ben said, infusing his voice with command.

"Not going to happen." Henry was clearly unimpressed. "I'll take Marlee with me and slip around the back, see if we can catch anyone coming or going."

"Whoever is in there is armed," Ben reminded him, twisting in his seat to glare at the older man. "If anyone is even still in there. Whoever it was could be hiding in the woods, waiting to take potshots at us. Stay in the car."

"You have to cover the back one way or another. We'll keep low and close to the house. And we'll arm ourselves," he said, pointing to the firewood stacked in a rack along the side of the house. "We don't have time to wait on anyone else. I promise we won't do anything risky." He slid across the seat and tugged on the handle. When nothing happened, he looked up, incredulous. "Are you kidding me?"

"For the record, either of you step foot out of this car, I'll arrest you. Stay put," he ordered, popping the snap on his gun belt. He opened the car door and stepped onto the forest floor as silently as a thick layer of needles and twigs would allow.

He closed the door and saw Marlee shaking her head, her eyes wide with fear. When the latch caught, she pressed her open palm to the glass. Sparing the cabin a quick glance, he pressed his palm to the exterior of the window. He hoped his gaze conveyed his unspoken promise to return to her and say all the things they needed to say, because he didn't have time to say them now. Unholstering his weapon as he walked, he cautiously made his way toward the door.

He was about to peek through the edge of the first window he came to when he heard the unmistakable sound of a car door opening. He angled his head enough to see Marlee liberating her father from the rear seat of his patrol car and bit back a groan of despair. When she gestured toward the cord of firewood, he gave an impatient wave, trying to shoo them back to the car, but they kept coming.

"Two peas in a pod," he muttered under his breath.

Fixing his attention to the window, he angled for a peek inside. The place looked to be one big room. The back of a leather sofa served as the dividing line between the living and sleeping areas. He could see the small kitchen in the far corner and a closed door he assumed must be a bathroom. Hoping to get a better look at the living room through the sidelight by the front door, he shuffled his feet along the planks of the wood decking fronting the cabin.

He peeked around the edge of the window and saw

a man clad in camouflage hunting pants sprawled on the floor, foot lolling to the side. He blinked, willing his focus to sharpen as he cataloged the other features of the room. The body lay between the big leather sofa and a stone-fireplace hearth. He allowed his gaze to track over the long expanse of leather inch by inch until he found the spot again. Something shiny gleamed in the dull light. No, not shiny. Wet. And dark.

Blood.

The body lay too far away from the sofa for the blood to be his, if he was gauging the distance correctly. The blood had to have come from somewhere else. He was still searching for the source when a hand rose above the sofa. A hand covered in blood. There was someone on that sofa.

Gripping his weapon in both hands, Ben flattened himself against the log wall and shouted, "Masters County Sheriff!"

Thrumming heartbeats passed, then a thin, reedy voice called out, "Help... Help me."

Weapon pointed at the wood deck, he reached out to test the door. Unlocked. The hinges creaked as it swung open. "Masters County Sheriff," he called again. "If you're armed, drop your weapon!"

"Help," the man called, his voice slightly stronger. "Sheriff."

Despite the warm evening, gooseflesh rose on his arms. Drawing closer, his grip on his gun tightened as he peered through the crack in the door. The man's annoying drawl was all too familiar.

"Thomason, I'm coming in. If you have a weapon, I suggest you drop it."

"Make sure he's dead first," the man said in a ragged whisper.

Galvanized by the response, Ben kicked the door in and burst into the room, his weapon sighted on the sofa. "Drop it now."

Panic raised the other man's voice an octave. "Make…sure."

Ben placed one foot in front of the other, never taking his eyes off the spot where he'd located Will Thomason's bloody hand. "Drop. It."

"He's dead. He has to be dead," Will insisted.

Ben flicked a glance at the man crumpled face-first and bleeding profusely on a cowhide-print rug. In two strides, he loomed over the back of the couch, his gun trained on Thomason. Bright red blood soaked the front of his shirt. He held his left hand to the side of his neck and gripped an old-fashioned revolver in his right. Judging by the man's weakness and the amount of blood seeping through his fingers, Ben worried one of the bullets had at least nicked an artery.

"He's dead," Ben said, willing the injured man on the sofa to drop the damn gun so he could assess the situation better. "Drop it."

Thomason blew out a breath and let the gun fall from his limp hand to the floor.

Then, and only then, did Ben give the other man more than a passing glance. "Who's the corpse?" He eyed the prone body.

"Bake…he did it. He made 'em," Will panted, his

voice weakening to a whisper. "I tried to tell him to stop, but he said…"

His voice trailed off. Circling the end of the couch, he moved closer to Will. With a firm grip on his gun, he nudged his hand under Will's and took over applying pressure to the wound. The blood flowed warm and steady, and the man's breathing grew more and more rapid. "He said what?"

"Young, Aberna—" His voice slurred the last syllables together. "Too greedy. Cut."

"Cut of what? Greedy for what?" Ben's voice rose as Will's weakened.

"Made 'em. He made 'em."

"Made them what?" Ben persisted, moving to place himself directly in front of Thomason's glassy eyes. "What did he make them do?"

"Roooo-let. Summone taugh him…win…every time," he mumbled.

"Roolet? Roulette?" Ben's heart lurched, then sank as the story came full circle. "Russian roulette?"

Ivan Jones had taught his minions his favorite game.

Chapter Seventeen

The creak of hinges caught Ben's attention. Marlee saw his head pop up. A half second later, a gun was pointed in her direction. "Police. Freeze."

"Ben, it's me," Marlee called into the room. "What's happening? Are you hurt? We heard you shouting, then nothing."

"I'm fine. Don't come in here," he snapped, lowering his weapon again. "Go flag down the others. I need an ambulance. And the coroner. Get Schuler," he added.

"Is someone hurt or dead?"

"No! Do not come in," he shouted. "This is an active crime scene!" His voice shook with exertion. Whoever was on the sofa made a gurgling, gaspy sound, regaining Ben's full attention.

"Stay with me, Thomason," he ordered. "I need you to stay with me."

Will. Will Thomason was on the couch and gravely injured. She stood frozen in the doorway, her heart in her throat as she strained to make out what the injured man was saying. "Gree-ee," the other man murmured as his eyes slid shut. "He caugh 'em. Yuhn, Abernaf-ee."

Ben pounced on the gibberish. "He caught them skimming? What about you? Why you? Why Jeff Masters?"

The man's breathing became even more shallow, each inhalation labored. Ben was losing him. He looked up at Marlee, his gaze imploring. "Ambulance?"

Try as she might, she heard no sirens approaching. The look of desperation on Ben's face spoke volumes. If Thomason went, he'd be taking a whole boatload of secrets with him.

"Hang on," Ben repeated to Will, his voice shredding. "We need you, damn it."

Half a minute passed in deafening silence until, at last, the distant wail of a siren carried on the wind. "Here they come," she reassured him.

Ben's shoulders sagged, and he let out a shuddering breath. "Too late. Damn it," he cursed.

"Ben?" she called out as the blare of multiple sirens drew closer.

"He's dead." The pronouncement came out hard and flat. "And so's Baker."

She flinched when he raised a blood-soaked hand to gesture toward the space between the sofa and the television, but from her angle, Marlee couldn't see anyone else. "Baker?"

"Appears they shot each other."

He rocked back and holstered his weapon, oblivious to the blood. Marlee averted her eyes, her own clean hand flying to her mouth and pressing firmly to trap whatever it was rising up inside her. A scream? A moan? It wasn't important. Ben didn't need to hear it right now. Not when he'd fought so hard to get at least one person out of there alive.

Tires skidded to a halt outside the cabin. Marlee saw a deputy's cruiser and an ambulance parked close to the cabin. She ran for the door, suddenly remembering Ben's car and worried they couldn't get through. Then she spotted the SUV pulled up next to the woodpile. She started toward the approaching vehicles when she spotted her father in the sheriff's SUV, slumped over the steering wheel.

While Lori and the paramedics raced past her to the front door, Marlee picked her way down the pre-fabricated steps and crossed the thick carpet of fallen pine needles to the SUV. "Daddy? What's wrong?" she called out as she approached. The windows were up; he might not have heard her. Reaching for the door handle, she peered through the tinted glass and her stomach dropped to her toes.

"Daddy?" she cried, yanking the door open. To her relief, Henry fell back against the seat rather than into her arms. She gave him a quick once-over and, seeing no blood, asked again, "What's wrong?"

Henry's mouth moved soundlessly. His eyes were wide and scared. Her stomach sank as she saw the gleam of a thin sheen of perspiration on his forehead. The left side of his face seemed to sag.

"Oh, no," she said, running her hand over his damp forehead. "Oh. Oh, Daddy," she managed, though a hot rush of tears strangled her. Something she'd read in an article somewhere popped into her mind. "Daddy? Can you smile for me?" she prompted, her voice as tremulous as her own attempt to demonstrate.

When only the right corner of his mouth moved, she leaned in and pressed her lips to the slack skin of his left cheek. "Right. Okay. Okay," she whispered. "Don't you move." She made sure he was propped upright in the seat. Keeping her voice as light as she could manage, she nodded a shade too enthusiastically. "Stay here. I'm gonna go get some help."

Closing the door behind her so he couldn't fall out, Marlee sprinted across the scraggy yard for the back door. This time, she didn't stop at the threshold.

"Help. I need help," she cried as she skidded across the laminate floor.

Ben sprang to his feet, reaching out to catch her, but she shied away, freaked out by the blood drying on his hands. "Help. It's Daddy," she panted, shifting her attention to the paramedics who were hovering over Jared Baker's inert body. "I think he's having a stroke." The two men looked at Ben, and she snapped, "He's alive, but he needs help now!"

Ben jerked a nod, and the two men grabbed their equipment and followed her out the back door. Within minutes, they had her father strapped onto a gurney, an oxygen mask over his drooping face, and were wheeling him across the tree roots to the back door of the ambulance. While they were loading him in, Mel Schuler pulled to a halt beside them.

"I thought Lori radioed two dead?" he called out to them. "Miss Marlee, what's going on?"

One of the paramedics waved her into the ambulance. "Two inside. We have a live one, but he's showing signs of stroke, possibly hemorrhagic."

"Good God." Mel threw open his car door and scrambled after Marlee, squinting into the ambulance as the paramedic made sure they were secured for the race to the hospital. "Miss Marlee, is that your daddy?"

She nodded but could make no words come out.

The paramedic shot Mel an annoyed glance as he moved to pull the doors closed behind him. "We have to roll. We're heading straight to Putney Memorial in Albany."

"I'll call someone to get Carolee," the coroner/funeral director called after them.

The door slammed shut, and the man tending to her father called out, "Hit it."

BEN SAT OUT in the general waiting area at Putney Memorial. Hours had passed since the ambulance containing Marlee and her father had sped away. He'd sent Lori ahead to check on them, but he'd been tied up waiting for the crime lab technicians to finish up, giving a statement to the Prescott County Sheriff—since Thomason's land was technically on the other side of the county line bisecting the lake—and waiting for Mel Schuler to transport the bodies.

He'd dragged himself home then, all too aware he looked like an extra from a horror movie and wondering if the sight of him covered in Will Thomason's blood would be the only way Marlee Masters would ever see him now.

For months after the shootout in the abandoned warehouse, he'd only been able to picture the sick glee on Andre's face as he lifted his assault rifle and sprayed the agents swarming through the door with bullets. All traces of the boy he'd loved as a brother were wiped away. All he could see clearly was the expression of stunned betrayal his friend wore when he'd seen Ben's gun pointing at him.

It took over a year for Ben to be able to conjure any other images of his lifelong friend. Still, those gut-wrenching scenes played out in his dreams. Not once did he envision them shooting hoops or hanging out on his grandmother's porch.

Would it be the same for Marlee? Would she look at him and only see blood and destruction? God, he hoped not. But even scrubbed clean and dressed in jeans and a T-shirt, he still felt dirty. Because he was tied into this. Had their lives been on a collision course? One set off by men driven by greed, power and vengeance?

Propping his elbows on his knees, he rubbed his hands together and let his head fall forward. Would she figure out how long it had taken him to scrub his cuticles clean? If she hugged him, would she smell the coppery scent of blood? His own nostrils were clogged with it.

He'd had to be tested. A Prescott County paramedic had rambled on and on about the dangers of blood-borne pathogens as he poked at Ben's veins. There was no use trying to explain to the kid there'd been no time to pull on a pair of latex gloves, even if he'd had some handy.

"Ben?"

His head jerked up at the sound of her voice. He shot from the chair and covered the ground between them in three long strides. But then he drew up short. She looked worn and worried, and the last thing he wanted was to push himself on her.

"Hey," he croaked. Clearing his throat, he tried again. "How's your dad?"

She drew a shaky breath, then let it go as she flung herself into his arms. He caught her and held her as a hard, wrenching sob broke from her chest. Ben squeezed his eyes shut, his initial rush of relief swallowed up by sympathy as he leaped to the worst-possible conclusion.

Burying his hand in her hair, he gently massaged her nape. "I'm so sorry." He pressed kisses to the top of her head, and she cried harder, tears gushing from her eyes and soaking the front of his clean shirt. "Oh, Marlee," he whispered into her hair. "Marlee."

She pressed into him, and if he could have absorbed all her pain, he would have. Because he loved her in spite of his every effort not to.

"He's okay," she said at last.

Her voice was so muffled by his shirt, for a minute Ben wasn't sure he'd heard her correctly. "Yeah?"

"I mean—" she peeled herself away enough to look up at him "—he will be. We got him here fast, and they were able to get him prepped for treatment on the way. It was ischemic rather than hemorrhagic, so they're treating it intravenously. They think the clot is dissolving."

He hugged her tighter, unwilling to let her go once she'd come to him. "Good. That's good."

"He's asleep now, but he was alert earlier. Seemed to recognize me and my mom. Eleanor Young drove her here," she explained. "They're in with him now."

She tightened her arms around him, and Ben had to bite back a shout of relief. She was holding him as much as he was holding her. "Good. That's good," he repeated. Then, catching himself, he pressed his cheek to her hair and let out a sigh. "Sorry. I'm so glad you were glad to see me," he confessed in a rough voice.

"What?"

She tried to rear back to look at him, but he clamped a hand to her head and pressed her to his chest. "No, don't. Just stay."

Just stay. Two simple, seemingly innocent words. But he wanted her to do more than stay pressed up against his chest. He wanted her to stay here in Pine Bluff. With him.

To his delight, she reclaimed her spot with a hum of pleasure. "I should be asking about what went on out there, but I don't want to," she said, her voice husky. "Not right now."

"We don't have to talk about it. Plenty of time to sort it all out later." He stroked her hair, tangling his fingers in the thick locks and combing them through to the ends. "How's your mother handling things?"

Marlee chuckled as she ran the tips of her fingers up and down his spine. He curled himself around her, wanting to remain cocooned in the embrace as long as possible.

"She's handling things surprisingly well." She pressed her lips to the base of his throat, and he stilled. "I have a sneaking suspicion she's been waiting for the moment she could be in charge all along."

Snorting, he pressed a kiss to her temple. "I don't doubt it."

She gave his torso another squeeze but didn't relinquish her hold on him. They stood wrapped up in each other in the empty waiting area for several minutes. When they finally broke the silence, they spoke at once.

"Don't go—" he started, his voice low and urgent.

"I've been thinking—" she began.

They laughed, then separated enough to be able to look one another square in the eye. "You first," she said with a nod.

But he'd said all he wanted to say in those two words. He hadn't had a chance to think of a convincing argument beyond them. At least, not one good enough to put to a lawyer.

"No, you go ahead," he prompted. "What have you been thinking?"

"Well," she began, her voice tentative as her hold on his back slipped. "It occurred to me you have more options now. I mean, with Ivan gone, and the others." She ducked her head and cleared her throat. When she looked up at him again, she wore her overbright smile. It clashed with the sadness in her eyes. "You might go back to Atlanta. Maybe get your job back with the agency."

He searched those beautiful blue eyes for a clue as

to what was going on behind them, but she wore her poker face. Her lawyer face. She gave nothing away. Then again, if she didn't want him, would she have thrown herself into his arms? Sure, they'd been partners of a sort, but if she were truly done with him, she could have sent him off with a handshake and a hearty, "Thanks for your help, Sheriff."

"I'm not going back to Atlanta." The rough rumble of his voice was unrecognizable to his own ears. "And I don't want you to either."

"You want to stay here?"

He nodded. "Yes. And I want you to stay here. I want you to *want* to stay here," he amended. "I want you to stay with me."

She beamed, and this time her sparkle shone brighter than the summer sun. "You do?"

"I want to stay here. It's nice knowing people's names, and I want them to know mine."

"Well, right now they think your name is Sheriff," she teased.

"That's not how it will be listed on the ballot this fall," he said gruffly. "I'm hoping by then, at least some of them will come to call me Ben."

"I'm sure they will."

Tangling his fingers in her hair, he tugged lightly to get her attention. "Listen, I understand how you've always wanted to get out of here, but I think things could be different than you expect. They are going to be different. Your dad isn't going to be up and at it anytime soon, and with Will—"

She nodded, her expression solemn. "Don't forget,

Wendell's retiring and planning to run for a seat on the bench."

"You're needed here, Marlee. I need you here," he stated, laying it all out on the line. "Somehow, I've tripped all over my good intentions and fallen in love with you. Now, I'm going to show you what a selfish jerk I am and ask you to stay here with me. Stay here for me," he said, unable to erase the pleading note from his voice.

A peachy-pink blush tinged her cheeks. He took it as a good sign. Evidence that she approved of what she was hearing. When she tried to burrow back into his chest, he caught her chin and tipped it up so she could look him straight in the eye. "I love you, Marlee Masters."

"I've done nothing but stir up trouble since I came back to town."

"I noticed," he answered gruffly.

"Pine Bluff is a mess. Timber Masters is going to be a mess."

He nodded. "Yes to both messes."

"I shouldn't want any part of this," she argued.

The color in her cheeks deepened, and a surge of heat rushed through him as he realized her eyes were growing bright with unshed tears. "But you do. You want me."

"I do," she said softly.

Gathering her close once more, he fisted his fingers in her hair and planted a long, lingering kiss on her, bending her back to make sure she knew he meant it.

He broke the kiss, breathless. "Do you love me too?"

She gave a huff of a laugh, then kissed him again. "I can't believe you have to ask. I shared my onion rings with you."

"Say the words, Marlee. I need to hear them once. Then you can go on teasing me for the rest of your life."

Unwinding her arms from his waist, she wrapped them around his neck and pulled him down until their foreheads touched. "I love you, Ben Kinsella. And, because I don't want you to feel you have to ask for my love ever again, I plan to give you all the evidence of *that* you'll ever need."

* * * * *

Rising to her feet, Lori peered through the floor-to-ceiling glass walls into the reception area separating the county's legal offices from the law enforcement branch. She spotted them by the empty mosaic-tiled fountain. Two men, one nearly as handsome as the other, but both equally repugnant to her.

Coulter and his attorney, Simon Wingate, stood with their heads bent close to one another. Lori's lip curled. There'd been few sightings of the eccentric millionaire since he'd bought the massive acreage out on Highway 19. She'd heard rumors about the man being good-looking but… Lori narrowed her eyes. He wasn't just handsome; he was gorgeous.

Disgusted with the thought, she shifted her attention to the man's clothes. What did a man suspected of endangering young women wear to be questioned by the local prosecutors? Loose linen pants and a finely woven white shirt. And flip-flops. Not the cheap dollar-store shower shoes Bella'd been wearing. No, his had wide straps fashioned in supple leather. He looked like a guy on vacation.

The sandals were a sharp contrast to the impeccably shined wingtips the man standing next to him wore.

Simon Wingate looked every inch the prep-school-educated politician's son.

Lori clenched her back teeth and focused on the man in the expertly tailored suit. He was the light to his client's dark. The perfect foil. All warm, gold-tipped curls, crinkly blue eyes and sun-kissed skin. Lori was woman enough to admit her mouth sometimes watered when she saw Simon Wingate. Not today, though.

Masters County's newest resident had lawyered up and come to head them off at the pass. No doubt Coulter waved a wad of cash, and city slicker Simon had come a-runnin'. Judging by Coulter's unperturbed expression and the district attorney's abrupt halt to Lori's statement, whatever they'd said had worked. He was about to slither out the doors of Masters County Municipal Center a free man.

Don't miss
For the Defense,
available September 2021 wherever
Harlequin Intrigue books and ebooks are sold.

Harlequin.com

Love Harlequin romance?

DISCOVER.

Be the first to find out about promotions, news and exclusive content!

Facebook.com/HarlequinBooks

Twitter.com/HarlequinBooks

Instagram.com/HarlequinBooks

Pinterest.com/HarlequinBooks

YouTube.com/HarlequinBooks

ReaderService.com

EXPLORE.

Sign up for the Harlequin e-newsletter and download a free book from any series at **TryHarlequin.com**

CONNECT.

Join our Harlequin community to share your thoughts and connect with other romance readers!
Facebook.com/groups/HarlequinConnection

HSOCIAL2021